THE TERRIBLE NEWS:

Russian stories from the years following the Revolution

Collected & translated by Grigori Gerenstein with an introduction by John Bayley

BLACK SPRING PRESS

First published in 1990 by Black Spring Press

FIRST EDITION

Black Spring Press Ltd.
63 Harlescott Road
London SE15 3DA

A catalogue record for this book is available
from the British Library

Designed by Phil Baines
Phototypeset by Selectmove Ltd, London
Printed and bound by Billing & Sons Ltd., Worcester

ISBN 0 948238 13 5

'Congratulations, you've been cured.'

Viktor Ardov, *The Hypnotist*

CONTENTS

Translator's Preface

The Terrible News is a collection of Russian stories written during the years between the end of the Civil War in 1921 and the triumph of Socialist Realism in the mid-1930s. Its purpose is to bring to light some remarkable stories new to the West and capture the atmosphere which prevailed in Russia during and after the Revolution, a revolution which liberated the country from Tsarist oppression but which also left the economy in ruins and the Russian population reduced by some ten million.

A violent social upheaval of such apocalyptic proportions is bound to leave people in a somewhat bemused state of mind. If what follows is a way of life based upon a rigid philosophy, where ideas are more important than living people, then absurdity is bound to make itself felt.

Looking back on one of the most significant events in human history people seldom bother to wonder what that event meant in personal terms to its participants, both the willing and the unwilling; how it felt to have been raped by six revolutionaries or to shoot a friend whom the new philosophy dictated had become your enemy.

The absurdity of some of the stories in this volume is not an abstract literary stance but a reflection of the mental confusion felt by people who had set out to perform a major surgery on reality and had ended up by losing their grip on it. As some of the more realistic stories in the collection testify, reality itself became much more absurd than any absurdist could have imagined.

Whilst the subject matter of these writings was provided in abundance by everyday life, their technique had been developed by the adherents of the Futurist movement. In the last year before World War One, Futurism had burst upon the Russian cultural scene with all the energy of a teenage rebellion. There appeared a young generation of cultural hooligans frustrated both with the Tsarist police state, tightening its grip after the events of 1905, and with the deathly-serious ideological framework which had been imposed on Russian culture by the democratic publicists of the 19th century. The young rebels were out to outrage and ridicule everything held dear by their elders and 'betters'; one of their earliest manifestos was called 'A Slap in the Face of Public Taste'.

In 1914 Futurism's first theorist, Viktor Shklovsky, explained to his unruly companions that their appearance was historically justified. 'The old forms of art are dead' he exclaimed, 'because they have become habitual, and the habitual does not enter our consciousness. Only a creation of new unfamiliar forms can bring back a vision of the world and raise objects from the dead.' The Futurists found the destruction of the old forms a most appealing task, especially as it was in harmony with the general mood throughout the country.

In 1917 the Futurists were absorbed by Proletkult, a non-party organisation of intellectuals which aimed to develop creative activity among the working masses. Its leader, the philosopher Bogdanov, was a disciple of the German idealist philosopher Mach. Proletkult's philosophical credo was based on Mach's theory of the 'economy of life's forces', and Bogdanov claimed that the trouble with the bourgeois soul was that, having grown used to perceiving material objects in their familiar context, it had fallen into a slumber and was unable to 'see' things anymore—it was simply 'recognising' them. In order to jolt the soul into 'seeing' again, the familiar context of things had to be destroyed. Only then could 'the economy of life's forces' be exercised. Bogdanov identified the pernicious 'familiar context of things' with the entire cultural tradition of humankind.

A prime example of Proletkult's artistic practice was Eisenstein's 1923 theatre production of Ostrovsky's 'Every Wise Man Has His Folly'. As the text of the play fell under 'the familiar context of things', Eisenstein did all that he could to destroy it. As Shklovsky commented, 'The new form had not been found yet, so they took the old form and broke it the way a child breaks a toy.' The production looked now like a circus, now like a music-hall revue. One of the characters entered on a tight-rope over the heads of the audience; a priest, a mullah and a rabbi cavorted on the stage, pouring water over each other; odd lines from the play were intercut with slogans and lines from gipsy songs. At the end of the show petards exploded under the seats of the audience and the rabbi screamed, 'Religion is the opium of the masses!'

Within a few years such efforts at breaking the moulds of conformity found themselves directed not against the old rigidity but against the new, against the Bolshevik system itself.

The Bolsheviks announced that their philosophy was the only true one, the only reliable instrument for perceiving objective truth, and that whoever was against them was against reality itself—or, in other words, was insane. They set about organising the people's psyche in such a way that every pronouncement by the Party would be automatically accepted as true while all other pronouncements would be regarded as symptoms of mental disorder. It was at this point that the value of writers to the Revolution was felt. Through their talent, writers had access to the people's psyche. The authorities became possessed by the idea that they could 'educate' a writer to see the world with the eyes of a Bolshevik without impairing his ability to influence the reader's subconscious. When they eventually realised that in this process the writer's talent, that for which they had originally valued him, was destroyed, the realisation came as a total surprise to them.

Thus such writers as Aseyev, Ardov, Ivanov, Leonov and Slonimsky were eventually re-educated into colourless literary functionaries; the rest lived through the kind of nightmare which would have been familiar to an inmate of a Victorian lunatic asylum. They were told constantly that they misread reality, that their perception of the world was wrong, that they wasted their time contemplating their navels or 'standing before a mirror'.

It is not difficult to understand how a sensitive individual would begin to doubt his own sanity under such relentless pressure, especially as the pressure did not always come exclusively and directly from the Party but was often of a more subtle, diffuse nature. The nation, brutalised by the Civil War and sick to death of chaos and bloodshed, craved stability and certainty. The last thing the people were disposed to do was agonize over the meaning of what had happened, to 'wallow' in human frailty and the vagaries of self-doubt and psychological nuance. The version of reality offered by the Party seemed desirable—everybody was going to be happy at the earliest possible time. Those creative artists who had the nerve to doubt this marvellous outcome were looked on with suspicion and resentment.

They did not go down without a fight however. In the winter of 1921 a literary group was formed in Petrograd under the patronage of Evgeny

Zamyatin. These writers called themselves the Serapion Brothers, taking as their prototype E.T.A. Hoffman's hermit Serapion, who renounced a career in politics for the sake of artistic freedom and independence. Their manifesto, written by Lev Lunts and probably the bravest literary document in Russian history, stated their refusal to be told what, and how, to write.

A description of the situation faced by these writers can be found in a letter written by Zamyatin to Stalin himself in June 1931, a letter which was itself an extraordinary act of courage:

> For me as a writer, being unable to write is tantamount to a death sentence. Under the circumstances it is impossible for me to continue my work because no creative effort is conceivable in this atmosphere of systematic persecution which has been growing worse from year to year . . .
>
> I know that I have the uncomfortable habit of saying what I believe to be true rather than what is expedient. For instance, I have never made secret my attitude to literary servility, lip-service and dishonesty. I believe that it debases both the writers and the Revolution . . .
>
> The campaign against me has turned into a kind of fetishism: as in the old days Christians invented the devil in order to personify evil, so today the official critics have made me into the devil of Soviet literature. To spit at the devil is considered an act of virtue, and they are spitting for all they are worth. They find evil intentions in every story I publish . . . My signature alone is enough for them to proclaim my stories criminal . . .

By the late twenties the Party alone, or rather Stalin alone, knew what was true and what was not. So total was Stalin's faith in his grip on objective truth that he was able to tell Russian writers with perfect confidence, 'Write the truth. Reflect reality truthfully. You must understand that if a writer honestly reflects the truth of life he will inevitably end up a Marxist.' To ensure that such was the case, the 'education' of writers was entrusted to the secret police, the literary critics in plain clothes.

In 1928 the last of this series of independent artistic groups was formed in Leningrad. It called itself OBERIU or Union of Real Art. Daniil Kharms and the poets Nikolai Zabolotsky and Alexander Vvedevsky were among its founding members. The group was ardently devoted to absurdism.

Existing outside the official ideology, its members were denied publication but did manage to organise a number of public performances. Here is a witness's account of their criminal activities:

> A huge shabby wardrobe stood in the middle of the stage. A morose young man in a shiny top-hat with a curved pipe between his teeth was pacing up and down in front of the wardrobe. It was Daniil Kharms. He read a long poem punctuated by pauses during which he blew rings of smoke into the audience. From time to time a fireman in a shiny brass helmet appeared from behind the curtain. The audience found the poem impressive, if somewhat scary. When Kharms finished reading and took a bow the wardrobe door opened, revealing Vvedensky wrapped in a scarf, with a scroll in his hand. Unrolling the scroll he began to read. Meanwhile Kharms materialised on top of the wardrobe in some mysterious fashion, where he continued to smoke his pipe. Vvedensky's low rumbling voice was hoarse from incessant smoking. He drawled his verse monotonously, and the ending of every line was as monotonously repeated by Kharms from the wardrobe. However, the most original performance was given by the Red Sailor Krobachov. When his name was announced nobody appeared on the stage, while the sailor began reading his poem on the corner of Nevsky Prospect and Sadovaya Street! The audience was bidden to keep quiet during the reading, and was rewarded by the appearance of the conjuror Pastukhov once the poem was finished.

It was activities such as these, apparently, which led to the liquidation of Kharms and Vvedensky in 1942.

History proceeded according to Stalin's stage directions. In 1932 all literary groups were liquidated, and in 1934 the new Union of Soviet Writers was inaugurated. It was open to all writers, as long as they expressed admiration for the Party's policy and embraced the doctrine of Socialist Realism, the main tenet of which was that reality was to be described, not as it was perceived by the individual writer, but as it was perceived by the Party. Those who did not belong to the Union of Writers were not considered writers. The Party's control over the Writers Union extended from publishing policy and fine questions of style, to housing and food supply and from this point on there was to be scant record of how it really felt to live in Stalin's Russia.

The stories in this book, whether they be examples of absurdist or more conventional realism, offer faint but disquieting voices from the past, warning us against the loss of empathic imagination which results from the worship of ideas. We should listen carefully to the screams of Zoshchenko's hapless character: We're not in the theatre, comrades! The blood is real, and the pain is real, and the madness is real.

Grigori Gerenstein

Introduction

Russians need belief as they need vodka and bread. At any rate that used to be true; now it is hard to say what is going on in the Soviet Union: probably no one there knows exactly. A recent volume of stories*, most of which originally appeared in the influential literary magazines *Novy Mir* and *Yunost*, reveals in younger Soviet writers what seems to be a fundamental lack of interest in the life of their own time. Russian writers have always been far more aware of their culture and past literature than western—and especially American—writers have of theirs; and this has not changed: the writing of the past is still clung to, as if for those with pens in their hands it offers the only fixed point in a dissolving world. But there is no historic precedent for the mental climate which young Russian writers live in today. What do Russians do in an age of almost total unbelief?

There is no doubt about what they did in the period after the Revolution. They contemplated with horror, fascination and amazement the spectacle of their society feverishly grasping hold of new ideas and convictions as if life depended on it. The most striking thing about this remarkable and unusual collection of tales, most of which were quite unknown to me, is the feeling they give that these writers of the time were never taken in by the aims and pretensions of the Revolution. It is interesting that this should have been so in the case of short story writers and tale tellers, for novelists and poets were soon making efforts to accommodate themselves to the language and thought processes of the new age, and to write as if it all made sense. But the best of them were haunted by the contradiction involved. Mayakovsky, the poet most approved by Stalin, and whose verse most vigorously proclaimed a new dynamism, was brought at last by that contradiction to despair and suicide. Even Pasternak, in his poems 'Lieutenant Schmidt' and '1905', attempted

* *Dissonant Voices. The New Russian Fiction.* ed. Oleg Chukhontsev. (Harvill.)

to write new epics of the Revolution; but he was well aware that there was something false about them, the kind of falsity which is felt to be typical of the age by Dr Zhivago, his great subsequent embodiment of what he felt to be life's true values.

Unlike today's young contributors to *Novy Mir* or *Yunost*, the writers who wrote in the years following the Revolution the stories gathered here, did not respond to the collapse of the old gods with comparative indifference, even apathy. They were astonished by the changes; and astonished, too, by the atmosphere of absurdity and duality which those changes had produced—duality, because everyone was supposed to pretend that what was being said, written or spoken in the service and worship of the new gods was true, when all around was glaring evidence to the contrary. In the face of what free and independent intelligence must see as ludicrous contradiction, what response was possible? Not satire, for satire presupposes an agreement on the part of the satirised as to what constitutes rationality: satirist and victim alike know what is true and good, and the satirist is abusing his target for failing to live up to that knowledge. But what if all the communal values taken for granted in a society have been turned upside down? The satirist is as helpless and as paralysed as anyone else; and besides, open satire had never flourished under Tsarist censorship, and had even less of a chance under a hysterically repressive new regime.

That is why the writers in this volume turned to the methods of what has since become fashionably known as 'the absurd'. Zamyatin's story, 'The Epistle of the Humble Zamuty, Bishop of Monkeys' is a very different affair even from the black fantasies of Swift or Voltaire, writers who lived in an age of reason. It loses itself in the ludicrousness of what it generates. Zamyatin's futurist novel *We*, precursor of a genre represented in the West by Aldous Huxley's *Brave New World*, is a more powerful work than anything else in the genre because it represents what was actually going on, and what were the practical consequences of the new Marxist religious 'communality' preached by the Revolution. Absurdism here is not exactly fantasy: it is more the accurate recognition of what had become the reality of the times.

One should not, however, exaggerate the literary discontinuity involved. In its comparatively brief but glittering span, from the 18th to the 20th century, from the golden age of Pushkin to what Russians refer to as the Silver Age of the symbolist and futurist writers—poets like Aleksander Blok, novelist-poets like Andrei Bely—Russian secular and imaginative literature had always thoroughly appreciated the grotesque and nightmarish side of life, and of Russian life in particular. Potemkin villages, and the total discontinuity between theory and practice during the regimes of Catherine the Great and her grandson Alexander I, show that the world of Zamyatin's *We*, or the (to us) more familiar fantasies of *Brave New World* and *Nineteen Eighty-Four*, were never far away. St Petersburg itself, the new capital commanded and called into being by the will of Peter the Great, seemed to writers a dream, sometimes a nightmare city. In his marvellous story-poem, 'The Bronze Horseman', Pushkin evokes a picture of dazzling gaiety and animation in the snow and sun of the immense capital, dominated by the statue of Peter reining in his bronze steed on the granite embankment of the Neva; and goes on to tell a pitiful tale of the floods which periodically inundate the city, drowning the girl beloved by a young clerk who goes mad in consequence and mounts the great statue, shaking his fist at its rider. After which the clerk slinks off in terror, convinced that the terrible Tsar is pursuing him and hearing everywhere the ringing hoofbeats of his bronze steed.

The tragic young clerk of Pushkin's poem appears in metamorphosis in the pathetic hero of Gogol's *The Overcoat*, and the same kind of figure is never far away in Dostoevsky's evocations of St Petersburg and in stories like his *Notes from Under the Floor* (usually mistranslated as *Notes from Underground*). It is, so to speak, under the floor that much of the most typical and most engrossing Russian life goes on, as is amply shown in many of the tales in the present collection. Echoes of all sorts abound. In Andrei Bely's novel *St Petersburg* the thunderous hoof-beats of Peter's horse are heard incessantly. In Daniil Kharms's creepy little sketch, 'Anecdotes from the Life of Pushkin', the poet is written about in the most banal and anticlimactic terms, an under-the-floor-style imitation of the routine pieties of Pushkin worship which had actually increased in the revolutionary era, Pushkin having been taken over by the state as a dummy mascot and pre-Revolutionary icon, his poetry unctuously quoted in Soviet propaganda films by the all-knowing father figure of Stalin. Kharms, whose strange little stories and sketches are quite unknown in English translation, eventually overdid his violently idiosyncratic reaction against the stifling hypocrisy of Soviet life and his ridicule of the Soviet proprieties. As Grigori Gerenstein reports in his preface, Kharms and his friend Vvedensky went too far with their bizarre surrealist cabaret acts and poetry readings, and they were both liquidated in 1942. Kharms, whose real name was Yuvachev, must have adopted his *nom de guerre* because its sound is close to that of the Russian word, cognate with the Old Testament 'Ham', which means ruffian or barbarian. His father was also a writer of fantasies and a revolutionary in the Tsarist era: it is a by no means untypical irony that the son should come to have the same sort of view of the Soviet regime that the father held of the old order. As Gerenstein implies, the Futurists of the pre-Revolutionary era were just as uncompromising, and just as devoted to the pursuit of an absolute, as the theorists of the Revolution were to be.

And yet as all the stories in this collection show—and many of them are both hilarious and bewitching—Russian writers have never lost their sense of humour and their appreciation of the ridiculous. And this humour is not necessarily absurdist or black; it can be both generous and gentle. In his sketches and stories the voice of Zoshchenko often seems like that of an almost sunny and good-natured version of Dostoevsky's under-the-floor man, a voice whose sardonic edge can show itself to be as appreciative of the hopes and fears, comedies and mishaps of ordinary life, as are, say, Chaucer or Rabelais. And this despite the fact that Zoshchenko was a manic-depressive who several times attempted to commit suicide, and who ended his life dumb and apathetic, forbidden to publish and unable to write. Yet in the early years of the Revolution he had become the most popular writer in Russia. All Russians love a clown, and Zoshchenko's essential melancholy is the melancholy of Petrouchka in Stravinsky's eerily tumultuous ballet. Writers like Zoshchenko, the Petrovs, and Lev Lunts, seem to be excluded from that peculiar dualism which haunts Russian writing and becomes far more marked after the Revolution: the dualism between pretence and reality, between what is, and what ought to be. Even so talented and witty a writer as Slonimsky, who could produce a grim, lively tale like 'The Station Master', sought in later years, almost like a miniature Tolstoy, to reconcile a shrewd perception with 'the demands of the ideal', the need for honest men and natural sceptics to accept the dogmas of the Revolutionary doctrine, as Tolstoy had striven to believe and live by his own unworldly doctrines. In a famous essay Isaiah Berlin observed that Tolstoy was like the fox in the old Greek proverb, who really knew many different and contradictory things, but who was always striving to be and to behave like a hedgehog, who just knows one Big Thing. A strong wish to be a hedgehog, to accept one universal and indivisible truth, runs through all of Russian literature.

And it can lead of course to subtle, or sometimes not so subtle, forms of hypocrisy and self-deceit. As the philosopher Shestov pointed out,

Tolstoy's real views are those of a super-solipsist, a piercingly cunning interpreter of his own instinct for life—which is far from the way Tolstoy professed to think life should be lived. This was one of the themes I found it most profitable to explore when writing *Tolstoy and the Novel*, a study which seeks also to explain some of the hidden contradictions in all Russian writing. Historically it seems that Russian writers must have positive hope, must believe in a mission and a goal of some sort, even if, as in the case of Chekhov, it is the quiet sensible one of slow alleviation, modest progress. And while waiting for the great moment to arrive, whether it be the withering away of the state and the arrival at the 'gleaming heights' of socialism, or the Tolstoyan ideal of pacifist simplicity, or the Dostoevskian one of Orthodox Russia leading and inspiring a new Europe, so many Russian writers cling to what may seem to us to be an unchangingly Victorian attitude: the importance of maintaining the proprieties in the face of the facts. Pushkin himself once remarked that the real facts of Russian life are too unbearable for art to face. There may be perennial truth in this anywhere, but it has revealed itself more starkly in Russia, where the prescribed 'Socialist Realism' was, notoriously, simply a mode of artistic evasion, of mass escapism. In his moving and beautiful memoir, *The Issa Valley*, the Polish poet Czeslaw Milosz remembers a moment in the war when he was serving on the staff of a Red Army unit advancing towards the German frontier. A senior German officer had just been captured, and after interrogation the Russians gave him a solemn pep-talk about the decency and humanity of the Red Army, schooled in the high principles of Leninism, in accordance with which he would now be treated. The officer, who had feared he might be shot, brightened up no end. He was escorted out, and after a few seconds the bark of a submachine-gun was heard—one of the escort had finished him off for the sake of his watch and fur coat. The Russian officers inside the hut concentrated on their tasks, taking absolutely no notice. Milosz, who was later to join the Party and for a time serve the Communist government in Poland, never forgot the moment.

It is a moment which almost any of the writers in the present volume—Bulgakov, Aseyev, Alexander Grin or Viktor Ardov, Isaak Babel above all—might have perceived and fastened on as the occasion for one of their early stories. The remarkable thing about all these writers is how conscious they are—even, in most cases, so shortly after the event—of the way in which the Revolution had exaggerated this dualistic tendency in Russian life. Babel's brief little tale, 'With our Father

Makhno', is a case in point. A Jewish girl in the Ukraine has been raped by partisans in the army of Makhno, a famous Revolutionary leader of the time. The following day the young 'runner' of the unit, a comic creature with a kind of imbecile innocence about him, is remembering the event while the girl stoically continues her chores, glancing at him wearily from time to time. Her gait as she walks about the kitchen resembles that of a saddle-sore Cossack—a typical Babel touch. In 'The Street Walker', 'the chinaman', whose leather coat shows he belongs to the Bolshevik authorities, picks up the girl for a loaf of bread and allows the old man she lives with to sleep on the floor. In the night he commands the old man to get into bed with her, an odd instance of dogmatic egalitarianism which Babel obviously relishes, showing but not commenting on the fact that 'the chinaman' has no interest in the personal feelings of the girl herself. In 'The Dead Body', Mikhail Kozyrev (who in the twenties belonged to a literary group dedicated to getting rid of literary groups) produced a surrealistic tale which might have been written to illustrate the Russian formalist doctrine that literature exists to 'make it strange'. The idea of the story, and the body itself, certainly seem strange, bewildering and terrifying—like the new world in Russia. And that is the point of the story.

No wonder that most of the writers in this collection were soon in trouble with the regime, or that the regime itself speedily arrived at a new literary orthodoxy, whose purpose was not only to glorify the regime itself but to reassure the citizenry that everything was going according to plan. Now that reassurance has vanished, and it will be interesting to see if the young writers of today will find some new way of confronting the fact. They will certainly be able to explore their own individuality, which, as Gerenstein comments, it was the principal object of the Bolsheviks to destroy. 'The Terrible News' of Alexander Neverov's story—the news that God has been replaced by 'Mars', as the peasants think Marx is called—may find itself replaced today by some news which for most Russian intellectual cliques would be much more terrible: that there is no special point in life except living itself, so you had better just get on with it. We are back with Pasternak's *Dr Zhivago*, which has not long been published in its home country, and with the simple truth of the Russian proverb, 'Harder to live a life than cross a field', a line with which Pasternak ended one of his Zhivago poems. In their vivid, stimulating and unpredictable way all these stories are witnesses to that truth, and to the folly of a new system and a new God which tried to make it seem so simple.

Alexander Neverov
(1886–1923)

The son of a peasant, Neverov's real name was Skobelev. He was educated as a teacher and his first stories appeared in print in 1906. He took an active part in the Revolution. Some critics consider him to be the father of Soviet peasant literature.

The Terrible News

Old Ermilov received a letter from the town. The letter was from his son Serega, in a rough, crooked hand:

'Dear parents, mother and father, and my wife Lukerya Evdokimovna! I have understood in all its depth the prejudice in which you live, in your ignorance. Therefore I notify you that I have discarded the old notions of married life and offer you, Lukerya Evdokimovna, complete freedom of civil cohabitation with any man you may choose, according to the desires of your heart. Personally I refuse to abide by any laws of marriage and do not intend to return to your village in the foreseeable future.'

Lukerya read the letter. Her eyes filled with tears, her hands shook. Ermilov didn't understand a word. When the reading was over he held the letter in his hand for a long time, stroking it tenderly with his gnarled finger. His old wife sat by, smiling. She was pleased to hear the music of the incomprehensible words strung together by Serega. Small wrinkles of childish excitement played on her dark, wizened cheeks.

'I don't quite get it,' Ermilov said turning the letter over. 'He writes a lot of words but there's nothing to catch on to. Do you understand it?'

'What's there to understand? He's alive and well: and thank God for that. He can't come home yet.'

After a pause she added 'It's better that way: one mouth less. If we miss him too much we'll go and visit him.'

'He writes in a strange language,' Ermilov said. 'He's become a town-dweller . . . Blah blah . . .'

The two year old Manka cried in the heap of rags on the bed.

'Shut up!' Lukerya cried bitterly. 'Or I'll take you to your father. Your dear father, the miserable wretch whom I fed and pampered. Now he's fed up with his peasant wife, and he'll soon be fed up with his town wife too!'

She picked up the child and ran out of the cottage.

The old people looked at each other.

'What's up with her?'

Ermilov had a feeling that something had gone wrong. He picked up Serega's letter and smoothed it out.

'A heavy page.'

The old woman was upset. She peered closely at the letter she couldn't read.

'God knows what it says.'

They called Ivan Konstantinych, a serious business-like peasant who sang in the church choir on Sundays. Ivan Konstantinych delivered an unexpected blow to the old couple.

'He's abandoned you.'

'What do you mean, abandoned?'

'He's converted to proletarianism . . . a German faith.'

Ermilov's face became purple, his neck straining. The old woman froze.

'It's like this, you see: the Germans had a Karl, they used to call him Mars. Once, this Mars decided to set up a commune. His flunkeys asked him "How are we going to set up a commune?" "It's very simple," he said. "We'll take the land away from all those who have it. Then we'll turn all those who don't have land into proletarians." There is a little snag, though. Before you join Mars's commune you have to renounce your parents and divorce your wife if you married in church. By all indications Sergey Efimovich has reached this very point.'

'So he's renounced us?'

'It looks like it.'

'I see. This Mars has got him.'

The old woman began to cry. Ermilov climbed above the stove, grieving. He put his hands under his head and lay there until evening.

In the evening Lukerya's mother Ustinya came. She spoke in a high ceremonial voice.

'I have come to you, Efim Siluyanych, not with greetings and not with a bow, but with an orphan's bitter tears. My motherly heart could bear it no longer and I have come here to tell you straight: she will not work for you any more. I'm telling you straight, she will not!'

Lukerya's father Evdokim, a diminutive man with a huge beard, entered the house.

'Don't take it amiss, kinsman, if . . . that is . . . I've come to fetch my daughter's things.'

The old women fought over an old jacket. Ermilov kept silent. Who cared about a jacket when their whole life was being destroyed?

His neighbour Ershov, also an old man, dropped in.

'You too have been hit, Efim Siluyanych?'

'Our son has renounced us. He's converted to some Mars's faith.'

'I know what Mars it is. They've put his picture in place of the icon.'

'Is he a saint?'

'He's that alright! Seeing what fools they make of our people, all Germans must be saints. They've put a red flag next to the picture with "Workers of all countries . . ." written on it.'

'Ugh!' Ermilov grunted, looking at his fists.

'You can't,' Ershov said. 'You know what the law's like these days.'

'He's abandoned his wife and child.'

'They think nothing of it. Like worms they suck one woman dry, then crawl on to another. It's no sin according to their faith.'

At night Ermilov didn't sleep. His wife whispered prayers before the icon in the corner. The moon looked through the window on the emptiness of the lonely cottage. A peeling black corner gaped where Lukerya's bed had been. A cat sat there, its thin tail up in the air, waiting for mice to come out of the cellar. The icon showed darkly through its glass, and a bitter darkness filled Ermilov's heart. His life had been split in two. Serega sat in one half with his unlawful wife, shouting loudly, 'I've completely discarded the old notions of married life!'

Ermilov wanted to thump Serega but the German Mars didn't let him. 'You can't, old man, it'd be murder. You'd better step aside and observe what comrade Sergey and I are going to do.'

Mars embraced Serega and the strange unwedded woman clung to his other side. The three of them marched towards Ermilov singing, 'We renounce the old world!'

Serega shouted, 'I'm not returning to your village in the foreseeable future!'

When the old woman finished her prayers Ermilov said, 'Have you finished praying? You can start all over again. Our God is no more.'

The old woman didn't understand.

'What are you saying, Efim Siluyanych!'

'Our God is no more!' Ermilov cried hysterically in the silent night.

He sat on the stove with a pale distorted face, viciously hammering the flue with his fist and baring his strong yellow teeth. Then he grew tired, his head hit the wall, and he cried the piteous tears of a child.

1921

Evgeny Zamyatin (1884–1937)

The son of an Orthodox priest, Zamyatin was educated as a naval engineer. He joined the Bolshevik Party in the early 1900s but did not remain a member for long. His first novel was published in 1913, and during World War One he supervised the construction of Russian ice-breakers in the north of England.

After the October Revolution, Zamyatin became one of the leading figures in the revival of cultural life, but in 1929 he was attacked and vilified by Party-line critics. His books were removed from libraries, his plays banned, and he was denied further publication. In 1931 he was permitted to emigrate to Paris.

Zamyatin is known today mainly for his novel *We*, which was the inspiration for George Orwell's *Nineteen Eighty-Four*.

The Epistle of the Humble Zamuty, Bishop of Monkeys

My beloved brother monkeys! Abandon your grief and calm your hearts, be secure in faith. As a true witness I can now testify: all the rumours of impiety and godlessness in the land of Alatyr are lies which only those with bitterness in their hearts call truth. Moreover, my beloved brothers, many a happy tear have I shed here, for no land under the sun is more zealous in the salvation of souls, nor in the destruction of this transient earthly life for the sake of the future eternal one. A dream has come true: the entire land of Alatyr has been proclaimed an independent monastery, and all its inhabitants, from child to old man, have taken monastic vows. Their life has become a veritable life of saints.

There is no sensuality here; no cymbals, no worldly vanity, but in everything a graceful meagreness and poverty, as befits monks. Conscious that ornaments of the body provide solace to the Prince of Darkness, the local inhabitants wear sackcloth, rags, and hair shirts. They do not anoint themselves with fragrant oils and they do not adorn themselves with gold and precious stones; on the contrary, in their scorn for the flesh they even avoid ablutions, for spiritual cleanliness counts for more than corporal, and the softness of the flesh brought about by bathing is perdition itself.

Following the dietary wisdom of their elders the resident monks keep strict and unceasing fast: not only are they denied meat but also fish, and oil is given them but once a year. As for wine and liquor, which inflame lust and cause laughter and merriment and devilish pranks, they are given none, and the elders punish severely any layman who brings wine into the cloister. I have seen some monks secretly burning tobacco—that accursed substance—as incense to the Devil, but the elders are saying that they will soon put an end to this filth, for why should God's earth be defiled with that foul grass when it can produce grain?

Thus they fight the Prince of Darkness through abstinence from all the worldly delights. Nor do they forget prayer. I am ignorant of their tongue and the words of their chants are incomprehensible to me, but when I walk past their cells at sunset it is with gladness in my heart that I observe, as of old, the rows of amicable warrior monks, and hear their harmonious liturgical singing. And when the monks gather to hear their elders preach, and all of them devoutly take off their hats, that singing fills my heart with joy. If some ignorant foreigner or impious layman keeps his hat on, the monks, zealous in their faith, slap the transgressor's face as was once done to the evil-minded Arius. Truly, glory be to God, they are not short of piety here! They honour holy icons as their fathers did. On the walls of their cells, refectories, communal temples—everywhere, my beloved brothers, I see the faces of their saints, and though they are in simple frames, due to the poverty of the monastery, they are piously decorated with herbs and flowers.

The monastic virtues of old, meekness and patient obedience, are an ornament to the Alatyr community as the stars are to the garment of night. The elders wisely keep the monks in patient obedience, and to every word from an elder the monks answer 'Amen', even if, desiring to test them, the elder says they have three eyes instead of two. Unlike other heathen lands there is no difference of opinion here, but rather a unanimous flock. I have seen many monks of mighty intellect perform a penance of silence, although I am not sure whether they have sealed their lips of their own will or have had the penance imposed on them by the elders; it seems to me that the latter is the case, as I am conscious of the wise fear of the elders who protect their flock from ingenious temptation. Is it not better to seal the lips of one than to endanger a thousand by sowing in their hearts vain sophistry and heretical doubt?

Thus the monks spend the days of their transient earthly life in labour, virtue, unceasing fast, meekness and obedience. It gladdens my heart to see not merriment but grief and lamentation, for he who is merry here will grieve there and he who grieves here will be merry there. Is this not true piety? Is this not a model of monastic life? Is this not the pinnacle of Christian devotion?

Rejoice with me my beloved monkeys! It is not the clever scepticism of pride that reigns in this land but meek faith, not impiety but honest monastic life, and I, the humble Zamuty, am a true witness to it all.

1921

Vsevolod Ivanov
(1895–1963)

The son of a teacher, Ivanov left home as a teenager and wandered
throughout Siberia, the Urals and Kazakhstan, supporting himself by
working as a labourer, sailor, clown and dervish. His first stories were
published in 1916. In the 1920s he was a member of the literary group
Serapion Brothers, but by the 1930s his work was conforming to the
demands of Socialist Realism and had become relatively tame and less
interesting.

Father and Mother

I didn't see my father for seven years and it was only in 1918 that I saw him again. He came through the school fence to meet me, his sun-burnt lips smiling atop his thin bony body. He fingered the sackcloth of my trousers piteously, and began to cry. His face looked as if he had been crying for hundreds of years.

But he wasn't in my mind and there was no joy to the meeting. I kept thinking of the day before my escape from Omsk: carts with corpses stretched along the dusty, sultry streets. I had counted seventy of them and walked away. My friend, the melancholy visionary and truth-seeker Sorokin, had said, 'The White Czechs executed them.'

Perhaps they had been executed, perhaps they had died in battle near Kulomsin. They were carted away early in the morning, hastily, and the pinkish Irtysh dust settled on them, the same dust that settled on me. I was also a corpse, but an escaped one.

My mother had a tightly belted swollen belly and her face was faded like autumn grass. She looked at me quietly and asked, 'What's your name now?'

'Vasily,' I replied.

Scared, she fell silent: I had a stranger's name now. From behind her came the dull, idiotic giggle of my brother Pallady. Thin-armed and thin-legged, with a huge swollen belly (he suffered from an enlarged spleen, malaria, starvation), the whites of his eyes were bluish-grey, his pupils yellow.

'He-e-hee,' he giggled nasally, yelping.

My mother hid my gun inside the mattress.

My father—his name was Vyacheslav Alexeevich—fussing, showed me the provisions he had stored for the winter and, looking up (I was taller than he) into my eyes, said, 'We'll survive, Vasily Semenych, eh? With so many names you must be a rich man, eh?'

Three days blossomed with the smells of the Irtysh cossack villages: fat-tail sheep, salt-licks by the dry reeds . . .

I went out to hunt. I had ten cartridges. Having shot a bagful of ducks I forgot to remove the last cartridge. In the evening, as I sat in the lean-to writing a story, Pallady decided to amuse himself. He pointed the gun at my father and snapped the trigger.

My father lay by the table, blood on his sackcloth shirt. The whole charge went into his neck. Blue flies converged on the blood through the window. They fell on his still-twitching face.

Later my brother squatted in the kitchen cleaning raisins for the funeral repast. When I came into the kitchen he said, 'Vsevolod, want some raisins? They're big, eh?'

The ducks I had shot came in handy. The cossacks with forelocks ate them, threatened lynch law and, with curses and signs of the cross, turned away from Pallady's listless giggles.

They said to my mother, 'You two should leave here . . . Maybe your son . . . God knows . . . His father, Vyacheslav Alexeevich, loved the Tsar . . . God knows what Vsevolod thought of his father.'

Once again I escaped.

The steppe. The blue vapour of the sand. Dung. A prickly gobi bush on a sand-dune, a kite on the bush. The feathers on the kite's breast are crumpled, tangled—he's moulting.

My mother and my brother Pallady sit in the cart. My mother's name is Irina. Beside the road, felled telegraph poles, bits of wire—the Semirechensk highway.

Human guts on the bushes. They are dry: the wind and the kite rustle them. Thin dry strings of human guts . . . Who is going to play on these strings?

'The cossacks and the new settlers are fighting over the land. When the cossacks catch a new settler they cut his stomach open and wind his gut on a stick. He laughs like mad, and they laugh at him, and then he dies from laughter.'

'And the new settlers?'

'They also catch cossacks and wind their guts on sticks. So it goes—on one side of the road the cossacks hang the new settlers' guts and on the other side the new settlers hang the cossacks' guts. Look how many . . .'

From Genghis Khan's Mongols, from Tamerlane's Turkmen came the custom of drying the funny human guts in the sun.

A long Kirghiz caravan coming towards us. The unoiled carts squeak, the camels walk slowly and the people don't look at us but, obstinately, towards the west. When we pass them it looks as if they have no eyes—a grey blur.

My mother says to me:

'The Kirghiz are running away from hunger.'

'Where?'

'Who knows. Maybe to China, maybe to India. They hardly know themselves. They're just running away because there's nothing to eat.'

The sand and, for some reason, the sky above. It's bluish-grey, like the sand. On the bushes, like ripe pods, the strips of guts. We pass the caravan and go on. The same sky, sand, hills.

Behind us, slowly, hardly raising dust, the Kirghiz people, camels, carts, drag themselves on. In silence, without seeing anything. They drag themselves on.

We also go on. We also want to be silent but we can't: I know where I am going and my mother is afraid. She is afraid of the place where I am going, of the people I am going to. We speak hastily, she first and then I, and behind her back, his shoulders covered with a coloured rag, Pallady giggles and yelps quietly. The further we go, the shriller his laughter, 'He-e-hee . . .'

After a day, after two more days, in the morning and at night, it's all the same: the sand, the bushes, the Kirghiz people. One of their camels collapsed and they left it behind, as if they hadn't noticed. Three children in the cart—they were also abandoned. There was nowhere else to put them and people were too exhausted to bother. A woman slid off a cart and stayed behind too.

'Who is she?'

'Must be their mother.'

I stopped my horse, went to the Kirghiz cart. The Kirghiz children, their dry lips wide open, breathed into the steppe. The woman sat next to them with her feet under her, her dirty headscarf askew, her hair smelling of horse sweat.

'We're going to die . . . no water, no bread.'

I said, 'We must take them with us, mother.'

'What are you talking about? Our horse can hardly walk as it is.'

'We'll leave the trunk behind.'

I bent over the Kirghiz children, wanted to pick them up. Crawling, the woman clutched at her children and hissed:

'Go away . . . go away . . .'

I reasoned with her, explained. Twisting her mouth, she clawed the sand and looked with hatred at my feet. Suddenly she jumped up and scratched my face with her long blue fingernails.

Then my mother grabbed her by the hair and shoved her in to the sand. Clutching, scratching, they pummelled each other and I couldn't separate them. My brother, sitting in the cart and waving his thin yellow arms, laughed like a rat, 'He-e-hee.'

1921

Lev Lunts
(1901–1924)

Lunts was born into a middle-class Jewish family. He received a degree
in philology in 1918 and was a founding member of the literary group
Serapion Brothers, whose manifesto, written by Lunts in 1921, explicitly
stated the group's refusal to write for propaganda. In 1923 one of his plays
was banned in Petrograd and he left Russia to join his parents who had
already emigrated to Germany; the following year he died in Hamburg of
a brain embolism. Lunts is still practically unknown in Russia.

In the Wilderness

I

At night, making fires around the camp, they slept in tents. In the morning, hungry and angry, they went on. There were many of them: who can count the sand grains of the desert or the multitudes of Israel? Each one of them led his cattle behind him, and his wives, and his children. It was hot and frightening. Days were more frightening than nights because of the even golden light of day, which in its immutability is blacker than the darkness of night.

It was frightening and boring. There was nothing to do except walk and walk. From the scorching boredom, from the hunger, from the desert's desolation, and in order somehow to occupy their hairy, stubby-fingered hands, they stole from one another chattels, skins, cattle and women, and then they killed the thieves. Then they avenged the murders and killed those who had killed. There was no water and there was a lot of blood. Ahead lay the land flowing with milk and honey.

There was nowhere to escape to. Those who fell behind died. Israel crept on, and the beasts of the wilderness crept behind it, and time crept in front of it.

A man had no soul; it had been burnt out by the sun. All he had was his body; black, dry and strong; a bearded face that ate and drank, legs that walked, hands that killed, tore meat and embraced women. Above Israel there was God, all-merciful and long-suffering, just, kind and true, black and bearded like Israel, the avenger and the murderer. Between God and Israel there was the sky, blue, smooth, beardless and frightening, and Moses, the leader of Israel, raving.

II

On the evening of every sixth day, horns sounded, and Israel converged on the Tabernacle, crowding in front of the large tent of twined linen and dyed goats' hair. Aaron the priest stood before the sacrificial altar, black and bearded, in a sumptuous ephod, raving and weeping. Round him his sons and his grandsons, and his Levite relatives, black and bearded, in purple and in scarlet, raved and wept. Israel, black and bearded, in goatskins, hungry and cowardly, raved and wept.

Then justice was done. Moses, raving, speaking with God but unable to speak the tongue of Israel, mounted a high platform. On the high platform his body writhed, his mouth frothed and there emerged, together with the froth, sounds, incomprehensible but frightening. Israel trembled and wailed and, falling to its knees, prayed for mercy. The guilty repented and the guiltless repented because they were frightened. And those who repented were stoned to death. Then they walked on, to the land of milk and honey.

III

When the horns sounded, Israel brought to the Tabernacle gold, silver, copper, goats' hair dyed blue, purple and scarlet, linen, goats' skins, rams' skins dyed red, badgers' skins, shittim wood, oil for the lamps, spices for sweet incense and oil for anointing, precious stones. Aaron, and his sons and his grandsons and his Levite relatives, took everything that was brought.

Those who had no gold, purple or precious stones, brought dishes, plates, cups and libation bowls, the best oil, the best grapes, unleavened and leavened bread, cakes tempered with oil, rams and calves, and goats.

Those who had no oil, grapes, cattle or plates—were killed.

IV

When they had no more strength to walk, when the sand burned the soles of their feet and the sun their skin, when there was no more water, when they ate donkey flesh and drank donkey piss—then Israel went to Moses, and wept, and chided with him, 'Who shall give us flesh that we may eat and water that we may drink? We remember the fish which we ate freely in Egypt: the cucumbers, and the melons, and the leeks, and the onions, and the garlic. Where are you leading us? Where is that land flowing with milk and honey? Where is your God who is leading us? We don't want to be afraid of Him. We want to return to Egypt.' In answer Moses, the raving leader of Israel, writhed on the platform, frothing at the mouth and spewing words, incomprehensible but frightening. His brother Aaron stood by in purple and scarlet, threatening and shouting, 'Kill the grumblers!' And the grumblers were killed.

Israel went on grumbling and shouting, 'Why did you bring us forth from the land of Egypt that we should die in the wilderness? Why haven't you brought us into the land flowing with milk and honey, and given us vineyards and fields? We are not going on. No, we are not going on!' Aaron said to his Levite relatives, 'Draw your swords and go among the people.' The children of Levi drew their swords and went among the people and killed everyone who stood in their way. Israel raved and wept in fear because Moses spoke with God and the Levites had swords.

Then they rose and went on, to the land of milk and honey. Years crept as Israel crept, and Israel crept as years crept.

V

If on their way they met a tribe or a nation they killed them. Hungrily, like beasts they tore them to pieces, then they crept on. Behind them crept the beasts of the wilderness who tore and devoured the remnants of the tribes and nations as hungrily as Israel.

The Edomites, the Moabites, the Massanites and the Amorites were squashed into the sand. Their altars were broken and their sacred trees felled. Nobody was left to live. Israel took their chattels, cattle and women. They enjoyed the women at night and killed them in the morning. A pregnant woman's belly was cut open, her child killed and the woman raped until morning and then killed. The best of the chattels, cattle and women went to the Levites.

VI

Years crept as Israel crept. Together with the years and Israel there crept hunger, thirst, fear and fury. They had nothing left to take to the Tabernacle when the horns sounded. Israel killed its cattle and took it to Aaron and his Levite relatives. Those who came with empty hands were killed. More and more often Israel went to Moses and raved and grumbled, and the children of Levi drew their swords and went among the people. Children, years, fear, hunger; all grew.

VII

It came to pass that Israel met the Midianites. There was a great battle. Phinehas the son of Eleazar, the son of Aaron the priest, led Israel, and the holy vessels and the sacred trumpets were in his hands. Israel triumphed and butchered the enemy. Then they shared the cattle and the women. The best herd and the best woman went to Phinehas, the priest's grandson.

The morning came. Having enjoyed the woman Phinehas took up his sword in order to slay her. The woman lay naked. Phinehas couldn't slay her. He went out of his tent, called a slave and, giving him the sword, said, 'Enter the tent and slay the woman.' The slave said, 'Yes, sir. I'll slay the woman.' He entered the tent. Some time passed and Phinehas said to another slave, 'Enter the tent and slay the woman and the one who lies with her.' Then he said it to a third, and a fourth and a fifth slave. They all said, 'Yes, sir' and entered the tent. More time passed and nobody came out of the tent. Then Phinehas entered the tent, and the slaves lay dead on the ground, and the one who entered last lay with the woman. Phinehas took his sword and slew the slave and wanted to slay the woman. The woman lay naked. Phinehas couldn't slay her, and he went and lay down at the entrance to the Tabernacle.

VIII

Great madness and lechery began in Israel. The woman lay on a bed, and the sons of Israel slew each other at the entrance to her tent, and the victor lay with the woman. When he came out of the tent—he was slain.

A day passed and a night, and then another day and a night again. There was no bread but nobody grumbled, no water but nobody thirsted.

On the evening of the sixth day no horns sounded and Israel didn't go to the Tabernacle but crowded before the tent of Phinehas, the son of Eleazar. Phinehas still lay at the entrance to the Tabernacle.

The seventh day passed, the day of Sabbath, and Israel didn't gather at the Tabernacle, didn't bring offerings. The children of Levi came in order to slay the woman, but they slew one another and the victor lay with the woman.

The raving Moses writhed on the platform and raged and spewed froth and filthy words, but nobody listened to him.

Phinehas, the son of Eleazar, lay at the entrance to the Tabernacle and nobody looked at him.

Israel stopped and no longer crept to the land flowing with milk and honey. The beasts of the wilderness, that crept after it, stopped, and time stopped.

IX

On the tenth day the woman came out of the tent and walked in the camp, naked. Israel crawled after her in the sand and kissed her footprints. The woman said, 'Break the altars of your God and build altars for Baal-peor because he is the true God.' Israel broke the altars of its God and built altars for Baal-peor. The woman went to the Tabernacle, but at its entrance lay Phinehas, the son of Eleazar. The woman did not dare to enter the Tabernacle and she said, 'Why are you lying here like the dog of the desert? Come to your tent and lie with me.' She also said, 'Someone, kick this man!' Zimri, the son of Salu, the captain of the children of Simeon, came forth and kicked Phinehas. The woman went back to her tent. Zimri, the son of Salu, went with her.

It was evening. Phinehas, the son of Eleazar, rose and went to his tent in order to lie with the woman. Israel saw Phinehas coming and made way for him. Phinehas entered the tent and there was a spear in his hand. The woman lay on the bed, naked, and on top of her lay Zimri, the son of Salu, naked. Phinehas, the son of Eleazar, struck him with the spear above the sacrum and pierced his belly and the woman's womb, and nailed them to the bed. Then Phinehas threw the tent aside and Israel saw the woman and Zimri, the son of Salu, naked and nailed to the bed. Israel wailed and wept. Phinehas, the son of Eleazar, the son of Aaron the priest, went and lay down at the entrance to the Tabernacle.

X

It was morning. There was no bread, and no meat, and no water. Thirst, fear and fury awoke. Israel went to the raving Moses and said to him, 'Who shall give us flesh that we may eat, and water that we may drink? We remember the fish which we ate freely in Egypt; the cucumbers, and the melons, and the leeks, and the onions, and the garlic. Why have you brought us forth into this wilderness that we and our cattle should die here? Why haven't you brought us into the land flowing with milk and honey? We are not going on. No, we are not going on.' In answer Moses, who spoke with God, writhed on the platform spewing froth and filthy, incomprehensible words. Then Aaron the priest rose and said to the children of Levi, 'Draw your swords and go among the people.' The children of Levi drew their swords and went among the people and killed everyone who stood in their way.

It was evening. Israel rose and crept on, to the land flowing with milk and honey. Time crept ahead of it, and behind it crept darkness and the beasts of the wilderness.

Phinehas, the son of Eleazar, walked last and kept looking back as he walked. The woman and Zimri, the son of Salu, the captain of the children of Simeon, lay there, naked and nailed to the bed.

Above Israel, and above time, and above the land flowing with milk and honey, there was God, black and bearded like Israel, the avenger and the murderer, merciful and long-suffering, just, kind and true.

1921

The Outgoing Letter N37
The diary of a departmental head

3 January 1921. At night.

... I consider today a great day, for today I conceived an idea which is bound to bring me fame and earn me eternal gratitude on the part of grateful posterity.

I got up at eight o'clock in the morning. Here I must allow myself a short digression in order to put it on record that I didn't sleep well last night as I had been considerably stirred by the director's passionate speech and spent the night thinking about the new reforms.

I entered the office at ten o'clock precisely. To my extreme indignation I discovered that none of my subordinates was at his place of work. In order to ascertain the rightfulness of my indignation, I perused once more the order of the Head of the Ministry of Political Education of September 7, which states that work at the Ministry will be organised on new principles (not the new principles that were put forward yesterday but the old new principles), and that therefore every employee is to present himself at the office at ten o'clock precisely. Those who are late are to be sent to the Palace of Labour as deserters from the Ministry's work. As a departmental head I had considered it my duty to read the order to each late-comer personally, to which they had replied unanimously that they knew the order by heart. If they know it by heart, why are they late?

The day was fraught with trouble. For instance, I discovered that a woman journalist registered her papers under forty-two headings instead of forty-three. But the main unpleasantness occured at three-twenty-five, namely: the club instructor Barinov entered the office without urgent business in spite of the fact that the door is equipped with a notice, 'Do not enter unless on urgent business.' Having entered without urgent business he proceeded to converse with the typist, thereby obstructing her work. When I attempted to point out to him that such behaviour was unworthy of a communist, he told me to go to hell and that he knew a communist's duty better than I, as I was an office rat. To this I replied that I was an honest proletarian worker. To this his reply was, 'The hell you are a proletarian worker. Don't think I don't know that you worked for twenty years as a chief clerk at the Tsarist Senate.' Then I retreated to my desk and commenced to write a report to the Head of the Ministry of Political Education.

It was then that the great idea struck me. Namely: we propose to undertake a fundamental reconstruction of our Ministry of Political Education. But how are we to reconstruct it if the organisation consists entirely of politically unsound employees? Because of this reconstruction is impossible. But we have to reconstruct for such is the logic of revolutionary life. Consequently it is the employees who should be reconstructed on new principles, in other words, the citizens.

That was the remarkable conclusion at which I arrived on the train of my thought. The significance of my discovery became immediately clear to me. In great excitement I put aside my report and attempted to direct my attention to current work, but I couldn't.

4 January. In the morning.

Didn't sleep well last night. I have decided to submit a memorandum to the Soviet of People's Commissars as I am convinced that the reconstruction of citizens on new principles should be carried out on a national scale.

5 January. In the morning.

Didn't sleep well last night. I have decided that the reconstruction should be carried out on a universal or, in other words, cosmic scale.

The same date. In the evening.

The moment I got home I sat down at my desk to work on my memorandum. However, when I came to practical suggestions I was compelled to discontinue my composition as the train of my thought had come to an obstacle. Namely: I didn't know how and into what substance the citizens should be turned.

Just as I came to this point in my deliberations my wife entered the premises in a state of great agitation. Her cheeks were flushed and her bosom heaved. She informed me that a hypnotist had moved into our apartment building and that at that very moment he was demonstrating miracles in the office of the house committee. I objected that according to the appropriate decrees miracles were not possible.

On entering the office of the house committee I witnessed the following scene. The room was crowded with people. An individual of suspicious appearance stood in a corner and, waving his arms over the head of a sleeping man, demanded that he do this and that. I stepped forward and delivered a speech on the current political situation. Those present abused me with words which I am reluctant to mention in writing. The hypnotist fixed his eyes on me, which made me feel sleepy. At this point in the proceedings my memory failed me. When I regained consciousness I discovered that the audience was in a paroxysm of mirth while the hypnotist was smiling triumphantly. It transpired that he had put me to sleep and turned me into a donkey. Apparently I had brayed like a donkey and, when given straw, had eaten it with considerable appetite. Outraged by such an insult, I declared that I would report the hypnotist to the Cheka, to which he replied that he was not afraid of me as he had a paper from the People's Commissar of Health. Then I retreated accompanied by a sobbing wife.

The same date. At night.

This evening was a great evening for I found the missing link in my theory.

A donkey, I thought, is a useless animal. However, if it were possible to turn a citizen into a cow, the milk crisis would be resolved. Or, say, those sentenced to compulsory labour could be turned into horses and sent to the state transport agency.

All this was good enough for the politically unsound element, for the bourgeoisie and its flunkeys, because a cow, a donkey and a horse are inferior creatures. But what should we turn the honest workers into?

Here my train of thought was interrupted by the following consideration: do I have a right to resort to the assistance of a hypnotist and will his utilisation contradict the established philosophy? Then I recalled that the hypnotist had a paper from the People's Commissar of Health and my doubts were put to rest. New perspectives opened before my inner eye: the Ministry of Health introduces compulsory registration of all hypnotists, gives short courses in hypnosis and produces crack hypnotists who are put at the disposal of the highest authorities.

6 January. After work.

At two o'clock the Head of the Ministry of Political Education summoned us, responsible executives, to his office in order to familiarise us with his Project of Reconstruction of the Ministry on New Principles.

The essence of the Project was as follows. It was based on the initiative of the masses, which was to be stimulated by the abolition of the Institute of Executives. The Head of the Ministry would remain while all the heads of departments, sub-departments, sections and sub-sections were to be re-named Senior Instructors. Thus the Ministry would achieve a closer contact with the masses, who mistrusted the Executives. The Project was met with great enthusiasm. Furthermore, there was to be a reform of the filing system, which would involve a 40% increase in the number of files. The number of forms to be filled in by every employee was to be increased from 10 to 16. Furthermore, all conferences between the employees were to be abolished and all communication between them was to be carried out in the form of written reports which were to be filed under special numbers.

The meeting received all these suggestions with great delight. Only the club instructor Barinov objected that the new principles would result in nothing but a new load of paper-work. Then, despite the indignation that was choking me, I took the floor and in curt and powerful expressions accused the club instructor Barinov of harbouring a bourgeois philosophy, as correct filing based on correct paper-work is the basis of Socialist construction, therefore paper is . . . but here my voice faltered and I lost my faculty of speech because at that moment a great thought occured to me.

The superior substance into which the citizens should be transformed is paper. I immediately entered this idea in my memorandum, supporting it with the following arguments: firstly— paper is a superior substance; secondly—it lends itself to easy registration; thirdly— paper is a substance, therefore it is useful to Soviet Russia in its present state of economic crisis.

I went on to expound my practical suggestions. My enthusiasm grew, words sang under my pen and fused into marvellous harmony. I was becoming a poet. A multitude of advantages on a cosmic scale presented themselves to my inspired imagination.

First of all: the struggle at the front would be considerably facilitated. For instance, the commander of a regiment or even of a whole army could turn his Red soldiers into pieces of paper and pack them into a suitcase. Having smuggled the suitcase behind the White bandits' lines, he could turn the pieces of paper back into soldiers and strike at the enemy from behind.

Secondly: the food and fuel crisis would be resolved since paper has none of the requirements peculiar to man. Under the same heading one could enter our struggle against criminals and women who are not involved in honest labour.

Finally: the paper crisis would be resolved as citizens could be utilised as paper in the true sense of the word.

This was the general drift of my deliberations. Completing my memorandum I went home. My wife asked me why I was so pale but I didn't answer her as, although a supporter of the equality of women, I consider their substance inferior to men's and propose to turn them into a paper of inferior quality.

7 January.

I suspect that the club instructor Barinov suspects something. I must be careful.

8 January.

Didn't sleep well last night, thinking what to do next. No solution presented itself.

9 January. In the evening.

Today during office hours I had an idea. What if I hypnotise myself and turn myself into paper? In extreme agitation I hastened after work to see the hypnotist with a view to receiving the necessary instructions, which he supplied with readiness. It transpired that in order to turn into some substance you had to spend a long time thinking that you were that substance. The experiment required continuous practise, silence and solitude. You had to think for three or four hours at a stretch.

10 January. In the morning.

I have encountered an unforeseen and fundamental obstacle. Namely: the transformation requires three or four hours of complete silence. My wife, being of an inferior substance, is unable to keep silent for more than three or four minutes at a time. I hoped that at night while she was asleep I would make my first attempt, but my wife, even in her deepest sleep, obstructed the experiment by snoring. I waited until four o'clock in the morning hoping that she would subside, but, being worn out by the excitements of the previous day, I fell asleep myself without noticing it.

The same day. In the evening.

On coming home after work I sent my wife to see her mother with the intention of continuing my efforts in her absence. As soon as she left I began to think that I was paper. However, paper is a rather vague notion embracing a variety of images, some of them quite indecent, and thinking of paper in general is an uncomfortable activity. Therefore I decided to concentrate on a specific article of paper production. After serious thought I chose an ingoing or an outgoing letter because they are the most subtle, the most ethereal phenomena. Some time passed and suddenly I felt rustling in my left leg. This affected me to such an extent that I jumped up, thereby ruining the experiment. But it was a beginning. I need more self-control.

11 January. In the evening.
Today I achieved further success. There was rustling in both my legs and in the left side of my abdomen. The rustling spread into my fingers, but my wife came home and spoiled everything. I don't know what to do.

12 January. In the morning.
Didn't sleep well, thinking what to do. Then I had a brilliant idea. Tonight I am on duty at the Ministry where I shall turn into paper, as turning into paper at home is too troublesome. Firstly: my wife never leaves home for more than three hours at a time. Secondly: even if I did turn into paper at home, what would I do then? The appearance of an outgoing document in our conjugal bed may arouse my wife's suspicions. Both these complications are removed if the experiment is carried out at the Ministry of Political Education.

12 January. Ministry of Political Education. At night.
My hand trembles as I write these words. I am about to commence the final experiment. I am alone in the building. The wind howls outside and the fire crackles in the fireplace. My soul is full of heavenly visions, my heart beats like a clock and my chest is constricted.

I have decided to lie down on my superior's desk so, when I have turned into an outgoing letter, I will be where an outgoing letter is supposed to be. I cannot stand disorder.

I will not turn into an outgoing letter itself but into its file-copy. An outgoing letter is bound to leave the Ministry, which eventuality I consider undesirable.

13 January. At dawn.
The great event has taken place. I have become a sheet of paper. The sun floods the room with the rays of sunrise, the birds chirp outside and my paper soul is full of joy.

I have a feeling there is something written on me. After a few attempts, overcoming all the attendant difficulties, I manage to read myself, thereby solving a great riddle posed by a foreign philosopher; 'Peruse yourself and you will know who you are.'

> File-copy
> Russian Soviet Federal Socialist Republic. Ministry of Political Education.
>
> 13 January. N37.
> Petrograd Commune. Distribution Department.
>
>   The Ministry of Political Education hereby notifies you that the 2.268 pounds of potatoes sent by you, for distribution to the employees of the Ministry of Political Education in accordance with the home front ration, have arrived in the most inedible condition.
>
> Head of the Ministry of Political Education (signature)
> Secretary   (signature)

On perusing the above document I broke out in a cold sweat for the following reason: if I was the file-copy of an outgoing letter, why was I lying on the desk of the head of the Ministry when a file-copy was supposed to be in a special file? It goes without saying that had I been in a human shape or, in other words, in the shape of a departmental head, I should have restored order immediately. Now I feared that the file-copy might be mislaid.

I could hear the cleaning ladies behind the wall. The office hours were about to begin.

The same date. In the evening.

I am writing this while lying on the floor, in which position I find myself for the following reason:

At three o'clock the head of the Ministry held a general meeting of the employees to discuss matters concerning trade unions. When the comrades began to leave the office a great misfortune befell me. The club instructor Barinov brushed me off the desk with his sleeve and, when I fell to the floor, stepped on me, thereby causing me severe pain. However, this severe pain was drowned by a still more severe anxiety regarding the fate of the file-copy N37 as, lying on the floor, it was in danger of being thrown into the wastepaper basket. Moreover, I recalled that it was the club instructor Barinov's turn to do a night duty at the Ministry. What if he suspected that the file-copy N37 was the head of his department? Hating me the way he does, he could cause me considerable discomfort.

In view of the above considerations I decided to turn back into a human shape and began to think that I was a human being. But soon I was struck by a thought which caused me to break out in a cold sweat. Namely: if I turned back into a human being the file-copy N37 would disappear. As a departmental head I could not allow such disorder. Therefore I decided to postpone a reverse transformation.

The same date. At night.
   It is dark. Silence. A clock is ticking on the wall. The club instructor Barinov has gone. He must have left his post. I will report this to the head of the Ministry.
   My soul is full of light and joy. Now there can be no doubt as to the validity of my discovery. I have been a paper for almost an entire day and I have not felt hunger or thirst or any other need peculiar to a human being in a human shape.
   A chain of noble thoughts passes before my radiant inner eye.
   All people are equal or, in other words, all people are papers. Man's ideal has been attained.
   Just as my thoughts reach this exalted point I see someone bending over me. It is the club instructor Barinov. He is looking for something.
   'Ah, here we are!'
   He takes me by the head or, in other words, by the corner of the paper, and fingers me.
   'Soft paper. It'll do.'
   With these words he picks me up and . . .

   Here, for an unknown reason, ends the diary of the departmental head. The latter disappeared without a trace. All efforts to find him were unsuccessful.

1921

Mikhail Bulgakov (1891–1940)

Bulgakov was born in 1891, the son of a professor at the Kiev Theological Academy. He graduated as a doctor in 1916 but his first publications appeared in 1919 and the following year he gave up the practice of medicine to devote himself to journalism and literature.

His first major work was *The White Guard*, which was dramatised in 1926 under the title 'The Days of the Turbins' but later suppressed. Stalin played cat and mouse with Bulgakov, now banning, now allowing his plays, and in his desperation Bulgakov even wrote a laudatory play about Stalin's childhood. Eventually he begged to be allowed to emigrate; Stalin telephoned him personally and refused the request, but lifted the ban on 'The Days of the Turbins'.

In 1937 Bulgakov was afflicted with neurosclerosis, the disease which had killed his father. The following year, however, he completed his masterpiece, *The Master and Margarita*. He went blind in 1939 and died in 1940.

The Red Crown
Historia morbi

The things I hate most are the sun, loud human voices, and a certain rattling sound. A quick, quick rattle. I am scared of people so much that I begin to scream when I hear strange footsteps and voices outside my room. For that reason I've been given a special quiet room, the best one, at the very end of the corridor, N27. Nobody can enter my room. In order to make my safety complete I pestered Ivan Vasilyevich (I even cried before him) to give me a typewritten document. In the end he gave me one saying that I was under his protection and nobody had the right to take me away. I made it quite clear that I didn't have much faith in the power of his signature. Then he made the professor sign it too and attached a round blue seal to it. That was better. I could mention a lot of cases when people only remained alive because they had in their pockets a paper with a round seal. True, that worker in Berdyansk with a soot smudge on his cheek was hanged on a lamp-post because a crumpled paper with a seal was found in his boot. But that was a different matter altogether. He was a criminal Bolshevik and his blue seal was a criminal one. Because of it he landed up on a lamp-post. A lamp-post was the reason for my illness (-don't worry, I know all too well I'm ill).

In fact something happened to me before Kolya's accident. I walked away in order not to see a man being hanged and fear walked away with me, in my shaking legs. Of course, I couldn't help it then, but now I would've said boldly, 'General, you're a beast. Don't you dare hang people.'

As you can see I am no coward. I insisted on a seal not because I was scared of death. Oh no, I am not scared of death. I am going to shoot myself, and pretty soon too, because Kolya is driving me crazy. I'll do it myself in order not to see or hear Kolya ever again.

But the thought that other people may come in and . . . No. I'd hate that.

I spend whole days lying on my bed and looking out of the window. There is a gap of sky over our garden and beyond it a huge building of seven storeys, its blind, windowless wall turned towards me. It has a huge rusty square on it, a shop sign, 'Dental Laboratory'. In white letters. First I hated it. Then I got used to it and were they to take it off now I'd miss it. All day long it glares there and I concentrate my attention on it while I think various important thoughts. But then the evening comes. The cupola of the sky grows dark, the white letters disappear. I turn grey, dissolve in the darkening air, and my thoughts also dissolve. The dusk is a terrible and significant time of day. Everything grows dark, becomes confused. The ginger cat roams the corridors on its velvet paws and from time to time I scream. But I won't let them turn the light on because if they do I'll start sobbing and wringing my hands. I'd rather wait with resignation for the last, the most important picture to light up in the dark.

My old mother said to me, 'I can't carry on like this much longer. I can see my madness coming. You're the elder brother and I know you love him. Bring Kolya back. Bring him back. You're the elder brother.'

I was silent.

Then she put in her words all her thirst and all her pain.

'Find him. You only pretend it has to be like this. But I know you. You're clever and you realised long ago that all this is madness. Bring him to me for one day. A day. Then I'll let him go.'

She was lying. She would never have let him go.

I was silent.

'I only want to kiss his eyes. He's sure to be killed sooner or later. Aren't you sorry for him? He is my boy. Who else can I ask? You're the elder brother. Bring him back.'

I couldn't stand it any longer. Avoiding her eyes I said, 'Alright.'

But she grabbed my sleeve and turned me so as to be able to look me straight in the eye.

'No, you must promise on oath that you'll bring him back alive.'

How could I give such a promise?

But, madman that I was, I said, 'I promise.'

My mother was faint-hearted. With this thought I set off. But in Berdyansk I saw the leaning lamp-post. General, I agree I am as guilty as you, I am terribly responsible for that man with a soot smudge on his cheek, but my brother had nothing to do with it. He was nineteen.

After Berdyansk I did what I had promised to do. I found him by a stream twenty miles from the town. It was an unusually bright day. A cavalry squadron rode in a cloud of white dust towards a burning village. He rode in the first row, his cap pulled over his eyes. I remember everything: his right spur slid down to his heel. The strap of his cap ran down his cheek to his chin.

'Kolya, Kolya!' I shouted, running towards the road.

He started. The sullen, sweaty soldiers in his row turned their heads. 'Ah, brother!' he shouted back. For some reason he never called me by my Christian name, but always 'brother'. I am ten years his senior.

'Wait over there by those trees', he went on. 'We're going that way. I can't leave the squadron.'

The squadron dismounted on the edge of the wood and we walked away, smoking hungrily. I was calm and determined. It was all madness. Mother was absolutely right.

I whispered to him, 'As soon as you take the village you're coming back home with me. Away from here, once and for all.'

'But why, brother?'

'Don't argue,' I said. 'I know what I'm doing.'

The squadron mounted and set off at a trot towards the black smoke. A rattling sound came from there. A quick, quick rattle.

What could happen during one hour? They would come back. I waited by a tent with a red cross on it.

I saw him after an hour. He rode back also at a trot. But there was no squadron. Only two riders accompanied him. The one on his right kept leaning over to him as if whispering something in his ear. Screwing up my eyes against the sun I watched the strange masquerade. He had left in a grey cap and come back in a red one. The day suddenly ended. There was blackness and the coloured headgear against it. He had no hair and no forehead. Instead there was a red crown with yellow shreds of skin.

The rider in the shaggy red crown, my brother, sat stiffly on his sweaty horse and if it hadn't been for the man on his right supporting him gently, you might've thought he was on parade.

The rider was a proud sight, but he was blind and mute. There were two oozing red blotches where his clear eyes had shone an hour ago.

The man on his left dismounted, took his rein in his left hand and gently pulled Kolya's sleeve with his right. Kolya swayed.

The man said, 'Ah, our volunteer got hit. Call the doctor.'

The other man replied with a sigh, 'Too late for the doctor. What he needs is a priest.'

The darkness thickened, consuming everything, even the headgear.

I am used to everything. The white building, the dusk, the ginger cat who rubs herself against my door. But I'll never get used to his visits. The first time he came out of the wall I was still downstairs in room N63. He was wearing his red crown. It didn't frighten me because he always wore it in my dreams. I knew for sure: if he was wearing his crown he was dead. But then he spoke, moving his lips iced with congealed blood. He unstuck them, put his feet together, put his hand to his crown and said, 'Brother, I can't leave the squadron.'

It's been like that ever since. He comes in his tunic with a belt over his shoulder, with his curved sword and silent spurs, and he always says the same thing. A salute. Then, 'Brother. I can't leave the squadron.'

It was terrible what his first visit did to me! He gave the whole clinic an awful fright. As for me, the case is clear. Just think logically: if he's wearing the crown he is dead. If, being dead, he comes and talks to me, I must be mad.

Yes. It's dusk. The important hour of reckoning. But there has been one moment when I fell asleep and dreamed of our sitting room with its old furniture in red plush. The cozy armchair with a cracked leg. The portrait in a dusty black frame on the wall. The flowers on the stands. The open piano with a score of 'Faust' on it. He stood in the doorway, and wild joy flooded my heart. He wasn't a rider. He was as he used to be before those cursed days, in a black jacket with chalk on its elbow. His lively eyes were laughing and a tuft of hair hung over his forehead. He nodded to me.

'Come to my room, brother. I want to show you something.'

The light in his eyes lit up the whole room, and the burden of guilt fell off my shoulders. There had never been a black day when I had sent him off saying, 'Go'. There had never been any rattling or black smoke. He had never trotted off, never been a rider. He played the piano, the white keys sang, there was a sheaf of golden light and his voice was alive and laughing.

Then I woke up. There was nothing. No light and no eyes. I never had that dream again. Instead, the same night, the rider in battledress came to me on his silent feet in order to continue my hellish torment. He said what he intended to go on saying for ever.

I decided to put an end to it. I said to him with force, 'Why do you torture me? Why do you come here? I accept everything. I accept the blame for having sent you to your death. I also accept responsibility for the hanged man. Now that I've said it, forgive me and leave me alone.'

He left without a word, General.

Then, bitter in my suffering, I willed him to come to you, just for once, and put his hand to his crown. I assure you it would be all up with you as it is with me. In a trice. But perhaps you are not alone at night either? Who knows, perhaps that man from Berdyansk with a soot smudge on his cheek visits you. If it is true, then you and I are getting our due. I did send Kolya to help you, but you were the one who hanged that man. By verbal order, without trial.

Anyway, he didn't stop coming. Then I scared him off with a scream. Everybody woke up. The nurse came running, Ivan Vasilyevich was sent for. I didn't want to live another day, but they didn't let me kill myself. They wrapped me up in a sheet, took the glass away from me, bandaged the cut. Since then I've been in room N27. They drugged me and, as I was falling asleep, I heard the nurse say in the corridor, 'He's hopeless.'

She was right. I have no hope. It's no use waiting for that dream—the familiar old room and the bright peaceful eyes. It's not to be.

The burden doesn't fall off my shoulders. Every night I wait with resignation for the rider with unseeing eyes who says to me in a hoarse voice, 'I can't leave the squadron.'

Yes, I am hopeless. He'll drive me to destruction.

1922

Mikhail Kozyrev
(1892–?)

Kozyrev studied economics at Petrograd Polytechnic Institute. He began publishing poetry in 1909 and short stories in 1916. In the 1920s he belonged to the Moscow literary group Contemporaries, whose chief aim was the abolition of all literary groups.

The Dead Body
A poem

I

When the day broke over the town of Vyshnegorsk, the psalm-reader Ignat woke up in the suburb of Pleshkin, the tailor Filimon woke up in Progonnaya Street and citizen Chizhikov, of unspecified occupation, woke up in the village of Fox Tails situated within a mile of the town of Vyshnegorsk.

Having woken up each one of them noted that it was time to get up.

The first to get up was the psalm-reader Ignat; he was also the chief clerk of the district executive committee. Looking out of the window he observed a grey horse harnessed to a cart walking driverless down the road. In the cart there appeared to be lying a man whose face it was not possible to distinguish. This extraordinary sight had no effect on the psalm-reader Ignat. Putting on his clothes he went to the district executive committee.

The next to get up was the tailor Filimon. Coming out into the street with no definite purpose in mind he noticed a grey horse with a cart walking down the road, and in the cart there appeared to be nobody at all. Reflecting that the horse was capable of finding its own way, Filimon returned to his house to finish the jacket he had promised the chief of the Vyshnegorsk police, Mishka Sych, who had enquired after the jacket the day before and was expected to collect it personally that morning.

As for citizen Chizhikov of unspecified occupation—who, incidentally, had served on the railway in the old days—on leaving the village of Fox Tails he saw that a grey horse had wandered into someone's oat field and was causing considerable damage to the oats.

Citizen Chizhikov led the horse back to the road and went on to Vyshnegorsk on urgent business which concerned not so much Filimon as the chief of the Vyshnegorsk police Mishka Sych.

That's all.

Except that that day in Vyshnegorsk people talked of nothing but the dead body which had been found between the suburb of Pleshkin and Progonnaya Street.

The first to notice the dead body was the psalm-reader Ignat. On his way to the district executive committee he saw a man lying by the side of the road who appeared to be asleep. Ignat approached the man and kicked him but the man didn't move.

'For God's sake,' Ignat thought, and went on. He met citizen Chizhikov of unspecified occupation and told him that there was a dead body lying by the side of the road, which didn't move.

Citizen Chizhikov approached the dead body and kicked it and, indeed, the dead body didn't move.

'For God's sake,' Chizhikov said. He met Mishka Sych, who was on his way to Filimon, and told him that there was a dead body lying by the side of the road, which didn't move.

Mishka Sych approached the dead body and kicked it and it didn't move for a third time!

'For God's sake,' Mishka Sych said and went on to Filimon's where he tried on the new jacket and found it well made. Only then, meeting a policeman on his way to the police station, he sent the policeman to guard the dead body found by the side of the road.

While approaching the dead body the policeman observed a man coming towards him, who appeared to be drunk and unsteady on his feet. Reflecting that the dead body was unlikely to run away, the policeman apprehended the drunk and brought him to the Vyshnegorsk police station. Then he departed in the direction of the dead body.

Meanwhile citizen Chizhikov, on his way to the railway station, passing the former house of the merchant Voroshilov, saw a notice nailed to the door of the house. It must be noted that the former house of the merchant Voroshilov was now occupied by a club. That evening at the club there was to take place a public debate concerning the existence of God. While citizen Chizhikov read the notice the whole of Vyshnegorsk was talking of the terrible discovery.

They were saying in Vyshnegorsk . . .

But what didn't they say in Vyshnegorsk! For a week they had been saying that a theft had been discovered on the railway. The value of the stolen goods was put at three billion roubles. However, the tailor Filimon arrested by Mishka Sych on suspicion of theft turned out not to be implicated in that particular theft.

When the chief of the Vyshnegorsk police, Mishka Sych, having drawn up a report on the discovery of a dead body, went to the village of Fox Tails and the psalm-reader Ignat was sitting at the district executive committee, it was twelve o'clock. At twelve o'clock the policeman sent by Mishka Sych, on approaching the place where, according to his instructions, he expected to find the dead body, found no body, either dead or alive.

That evening comrade Migai, a food inspector from Lykov, was released from the Vyshnegorsk police station as he appeared to have been apprehended by mistake.

II

Gavrila Terentyev, chairman of the Zashchekino village committee, came to the psalm reader Ignat, who was sitting at the district executive committee, and told him the following:

He, Terentyev, was sitting in his house in Zashchekino celebrating St. Elias's day when the peasant Stepan Paramonov of the village of Losnovo came to him and said that someone was demanding a cart from him, Terentyev, as he was chairman of the village committee. Then he, Terentyev, as chairman of the village committee, came out into the street and saw a citizen who was sitting in a cart and demanding another cart, to which he, Terentyev, as chairman of the village committee, said that no cart was available as it was a holiday. Then the above citizen, who turned out to be Mr. Migai, a food inspector from Lykov, inflicted an insult upon him, Terentyev, in the form of a blow to his, Terentyev's, physiognomy so that he, Terentyev, as chairman of the village committee, nearly fell off his feet, and therefore he requested that measures be taken against such citizens.

The above statement was sent to the chief of the district police Ptichkin to be responded to within a period of three days.

Meanwhile in Vyshnegorsk they were saying . . .

But what is not said in Vyshnegorsk when Grandma Fetinya meets Aunt Aksinya in the High Street not far from the church!

'The end of the world,' Grandma Fetinya says . . .

'He must've risen from the dead,' Aunt Aksinya replies, and they break up seeing at a distance Mishka Sych, the chief of the Vyshnegorsk police, who is coming back from the village of Fox Tails.

Mishka Sych visited Fox Tails on the following business:

In the morning the peasant Mikita Sedoy of the village of Fox Tails discovered that a grey horse had wandered into his oat field and caused considerable damage to his oats. Mikita Sedoy drove the horse into the pigsty. Then the peasant Ilya Khudoy of the same village came to him and told him that he, Ilya Khudoy, was also owed compensation for the damage caused by the horse.

Mishka Sych ordered that, until the case was decided, the horse was to be detained in custody at the Vyshnegorsk police station. He rode the horse back to town and it was only then that he learnt of the disappearance of the dead body.

'I'll get to the bottom of this!' Mishka Sych said and sent an investigator to find the dead body of uncertain ownership.

Meanwhile in Vyshnegorsk they were saying . . .

But that doesn't concern us.

On his way home from work the psalm-reader Ignat passed the former house of the merchant Voroshilov and read the notice nailed to its door, which expressed doubt in the existence of God. As a man who entertained no doubt in the existence of God, the psalm-reader Ignat prepared himself for the public debate by draining a bottle of illicit spirit obtained from the local bootlegger Butyagin.

The public debate took place at eight o'clock that evening.

The entire population of Vyshnegorsk attended. Despite hot argument it was decided by a majority of forty to thirty that God didn't exist.

Then the bootlegger Butyagin took the floor and said that in order to decide a question as important as the existence of God, the majority should be at least three quarters. The psalm-reader Ignat, beating his breast, said that in his breast God truly existed. Citizen Chizhikov, of unspecified occupation, said that, since he was at present unemployed and not a Party member, the whole question of the existence of God was of no importance to him personally.

As I say the entire population of Vyshnegorsk attended the public debate, and on their way home people talked of what had been the only topic of conversation in Vyshnegorsk that day, namely, that the chief of the Vyshnegorsk police Mishka Sych had got himself a new jacket from somewhere, the like of which he could not possibly have had before.

III

The peasant Stepan Paramonov of the village of Losnovo came to Vyshnegorsk looking for his grey horse which had disappeared. He also looked all over the village of Fox Tails. He was told that the horse was being detained in custody at the Vyshnegorsk police station. Stepan Paramonov went to the chief of police and demanded his horse back. Mishka Sych did not give him the grey horse back as he had no proof of ownership. Stepan Paramonov went to Lykov to obtain proof of ownership from the food inspector Migai.

That happened in the morning. At night the policeman guarding the place where the dead body had lain the day before saw a shadow slinking from Vyshnegorsk in the direction of Fox Tails. In ten minutes another shadow, this time riding a horse, proceeded in the same direction. Apparently the shadow was the soul of the vanished body, which wandered around at night in search of the body it belonged to.

Next morning Mishka Sych received, from the railway station, a report of the theft of a consignment of textiles belonging to the trade union 'Needle'. He went to the station to institute an enquiry.

Meanwhile in Vyshnegorsk they were saying . . .

Alright, this is what they were saying in Vyshnegorsk:

The previous night's decision to abolish the existence of God had thrown the priest Fr. Milovidov into such a depression that he, together with the psalm-reader Ignat, came to the bootlegger Butyagin demanding illicit spirits. When informed by Butyagin that he, Fr. Milovidov, had drunk all the available spirit, Fr. Milovidov shouted, with the help of a revolver, 'Tell me, you so-and-so, is there a God or not!'

The Vyshnegorsk bootlegger Butyagin readily testified to the existence of God.

The same morning the district chief of police Ptichkin received a statement from citizen Terentyev complaining of the insult received by him, Terentyev, chairman of the village committee, from the food inspector Migai of the town of Lykov, in the form of a blow to the head. He summoned Migai from Lykov and questioned him.

These are the circumstances of the case according to the testimony given by the food inspector Migai:

He, Migai, travelled from Razgulyaevo to Lykov in connection with the collection of the egg and butter tax. At Razgulyaevo they were celebrating the saint's day. The first village on his way was Vasikha, where they were also celebrating the saint's day. The chairman of the Vasikha village committee supplied him with a cart which brought him to the village of Losnovo, where they were also celebrating the saint's day. The chairman of the Losnovo village committee supplied him with a cart which brought him to the village of Zashchekino, where they were also celebrating the saint's day . . .

Then a drunken person approached him together with the cart driver, who was citizen Paramonov, and announced that they would not drive him any further. Migai said that they were obliged by law to take him to Lykov, at which the drunken person told him to go to a place which comrade Migai didn't know. Then an old woman came running, and some peasants, and the drunken person demanded to see Migai's warrant, while the peasants shouted, 'He wants butter—we'll give him butter!'

Then another drunken person approached him and he, comrade Migai, grabbed that person by the hand shouting, 'You keep your hands off me!' The drunken person shoved him while the cart driver threw down his reins and said, 'Drive it yourself!' This drunken person turned out to be the chairman of the Zashchekino village committee, Terentyev, who kept shoving comrade Migai and waving his fists. Comrade Migai could stand it no longer and he thumped citizen Terentyev, who fell into the cart, thereby frightening the horse who bolted and disappeared so that next evening comrade Migai had to walk all the way to Lykov.

Having taken this testimony the district chief of police Ptichkin wrote a conclusion to the effect that he had established that the food inspector comrade Migai had inflicted a blow to the head of the Zashchekino village committee chairman, Terentyev, but that, in his opinion, the above blow was due to the fact that comrade Migai had been the district's food inspector for a long time and was too well known to everybody, therefore he, Migai, as an honest and committed worker, should be reprimanded and threatened with court proceedings.

The file was sent to Lykov for further investigation.

Meanwhile the investigator had established that the vanished body could have belonged to nobody but the district food inspector Migai, who was duly apprehended and detained in custody at the Vyshnegorsk police station.

IV

Next morning the file on the food inspector Migai arrived in Lykov. The peasants of the village of Zashchekino, and the peasant Stepan Paramonov of the village of Losnovo, were questioned. It was confirmed that Migai had arrived in Zashchekino from Razgulyaevo, where they had been celebrating the saint's day, driven by the peasant Stepan Paramonov of the village of Losnovo and his grey horse whom he, Paramonov, needed back for work on his holding. Nobody denied the fact that the whole district knew very well who comrade Migai was.

As for murder, nobody had done anything of the sort, except that two men had been stabbed in Razgulyaevo but remained alive, and nobody had the foggiest idea where the dead body could have got to.

The file was returned to the Vyshnegorsk executive committee where it was received by the psalm-reader Ignat in his capacity as the chief clerk.

All that happened in the morning. During the night the police chief Mishka Sych entered Migai's cell and, boxing his ears as his suspect's status warranted, said to him, 'You killed him!'

Migai had no answer to that. Mishka Sych told Migai to show him where the dead body was hidden. After three hours of wandering Migai brought him to someone's oat field where, indeed, the dead body of uncertain ownership was hidden.

A policeman was detailed to guard the body. At dawn the policeman saw a shadow proceeding in the direction of Fox Tails. He was so frightened that he fell asleep. When he woke up he saw the psalm-reader Ignat sitting next to him arguing that, after all, God did exist, while the dead body had disappeared without a trace.

At the same time a report was drawn up accusing the priest Fr. Milovidov of armed extortion and of spreading false rumours of resurrection. The same morning the psalm reader Ignat was apprehended and immediately released as he was the chief clerk of the executive committee. The psalm-reader Ignat, badly cut up, said to Mishka Sych, 'I'll prove to you that God exists!'

Immediately, at the request of the district executive committee, there followed the release of the suspect Migai who had been mistaken for a dead body due to an error by the chief of police.

Meanwhile they were saying in Vyshnegorsk—and not only in Vyshnegorsk but also in the village of Fox Tails—that every night there was a shadow wandering from Vyshnegorsk to Fox Tails and that that shadow was trampling the oats of the peasants Ilya Sedoy and Mikita Khudoy so that the oats might rot as it was a rainy summer.

Ilya Khudoy and Mikita Sedoy lay in ambush at night—they lay within half a mile of each other. First Ilya Khudoy saw the above shadow and chased it but didn't catch it. Then Mikita Sedoy saw another shadow which sat in a cart driven by a horse whose colour it was not possible to distinguish. The horse walked right across the oats in the direction of the village.

Mikita Sedoy said to the shadow, 'Hold it!'

It proved to be the shadow of citizen Chizhikov, of unspecified occupation, and it was carting the textiles from the Vyshnegorsk railway station.

Then the tailor Filimon was apprehended, and the chief of the Vyshnegorsk police Mishka Sych confessed that Filimon had made him a new jacket the like of which he could not possibly have had before because of his narrow means. He claimed that, apart from inflicting violence on the food inspector Migai, he was totally innocent.

Meanwhile they were saying in Vyshnegorsk . . .

Well, they were saying the same thing in Lykov and Razgulyaevo, and even in Zashchekino they spoke of nothing but the discovery of a gang which had been stealing textiles from the Vyshnegorsk railway station, and that the gang was led by a dead body of uncertain ownership.

Next morning when the psalm-reader Ignat, who was also the chief clerk of the district executive committee, woke up and looked out of the window he observed a grey horse harnessed to a cart in which sat the peasant of the village of Losnovo, Stepan Paramonov.

1922

Isaak Babel
(1894–1941)

Babel was the son of a Jewish tradesman from Odessa and was educated as an economist. His first stories, for which he was indicted on charges of pornography, were published in 1916. Babel fought in the Red Army in the Civil War and described his experiences in his famous collection of short stories, *Red Cavalry*. Unable to conform to the demands of Socialist Realism he virtually stopped writing in the mid-1930s, and described himself as 'a master of silence'. He was arrested in 1939 and shot in 1941. All Babel's works and any public mention of his name were banned in the Soviet Union until 1956.

With Our Father Makhno

The night before, six Makhno cossacks had raped a servant-maid. I heard the news in the morning and decided to go and see how a woman looked after being raped by six men. I found her in the kitchen. She was washing clothes, bending over a tub. She was a fat girl with blooming cheeks. Only an unhurried existence on the fertile Ukrainian soil can fill a Jewess with such bovine juices. The girl's legs, fat, brick-red, swollen like balloons, stank sweetly like freshly cut meat. It seemed to me that all that was left of yesterday's virginity were her cheeks, inflamed more than usual, and her downcast eyes.

In the kitchen, apart from the servant-maid, there sat urchin Kikin, runner for the Staff of Our Father Makhno. He was reputed to be off his nut at the HQ, and he thought nothing of walking on his hands at the most inappropriate moments.

Many times I had caught him in front of the mirror. He would lift his legs in their torn trousers, wink at himself, slap his bare boyish belly, sing wildly and make triumphant grimaces, which made him split his sides with laughter.

Today again I found him doing something special. He was pasting strips of gilt paper on to a German helmet.

'How many did you take on last night, Rukhlya?' he asked as, screwing up his eyes, he examined his decorated helmet.

The girl was silent.

'You took on six,' the boy went on. 'And there are women who can take on as many as twenty.'

'Go and fetch some water,' the girl said.

Kikin brought a pail of water from the yard. Shuffling his bare feet he went to the mirror, pulled on the helmet with the gilt strips and examined his reflection closely. The mirror absorbed him. Sticking his fingers into his nostrils the boy followed avidly the alterations in the shape of his nose under the pressure from inside. 'I am leaving HQ.' He turned to the Jewess. 'Don't tell anybody, Rukhlya. Stetsenko is taking me into his squadron. At least they give you a uniform there, and there's the honour, and I'll find comrades in arms. Quite a change from the gang of rag-bags here . . . Last night as we caught you and I was holding your head, I said to Matvey Vasilich, "What's going on, Matvey Vasilich, four men have had a go and I am still holding her head. You've been twice yourself, Matvey Vasilich. You are not going to leave me out just because I am a junior and not of your company . . ." Well, you, Rukhlya, must've heard yourself what he said. "We'll never leave you out, Kikin", he said, "just wait till all the orderlies have been, then you can have a go". Like hell they let me have a go . . . Afterwards, when we were dragging you into the bushes, Matvey Vasilich said to me, "You can do it now if you wish, Kikin". "No," I said, "I don't wish to get in there after Vaska, I'd be sorry for the rest of my life." '

Kikin snorted angrily and fell silent. He lay down on the floor and stared into the distance, bare-footed, lanky, dejected, his belly bare and his helmet shining over his straw-like hair.

'People are saying all sorts of things about what heroes the Makhno cossacks are,' he said morosely. 'You just hang about with them for a while and you'll soon find out that every one of them is nursing a grievance of some kind.'

The Jewess raised her red face from the tub, glanced at the boy and went out of the kitchen with the laborious gait of a cavalry man who has just put his numbed feet on the ground after a long ride.

Left alone the boy looked round the kitchen with a bored glance, sighed, put his hands on the floor, threw up his feet and began to walk quickly up and down on his hands.

1923

The Street Walker

An implacable night. A murderous wind. The fingers of a corpse fumble with the icy intestines of Petersburg. Crimson chemist shops are freezing on street corners. A chemist drops his well-combed little head to one side. The frost takes a chemist shop by its violet heart and the chemist shop's heart dies.

Not a soul on the Nevsky. Inky bubbles burst in the sky. Two o'clock in the morning. An implacable night.

A girl and a person sit on the railing in front of the cafe 'Bristol'. Two whimpering backs. Two freezing crows on a bare bush.

'. . . if, by the will of Satan, you succeed the late Emperor, lead the masses, you matricides . . . But no hope . . . They depend on the Letts, and the Letts are Mongols, Glafira.'

The person's cheeks hang on both sides of his face like a rag-and-bone man's bags. In his rusty pupils, wounded cats roam.

'For Christ's sake, Aristarkh Terentich, step over to Nadezhdinskaya Street. Who's going to pick me up when I'm with a man?'

A Chinaman in leather passes by. He raises a loaf of bread over his head. With a blue fingernail he draws a line on the crust. A pound. Glafira puts up two fingers. Two pounds.

A thousand saws moan in the ossified snow of the side streets. A star glitters in the inky firmament.

The Chinaman, coming to a halt, mutters through his clenched teeth, 'You dirty, eh?'

'I'm clean, comrade.'

'A pound.'

Aristarkh's pupils light up in Nadezhdinskaya Street.

'Darling,' the girl says hoarsely, 'I've got my godfather with me here . . . Will you let him sleep on the floor?'

The Chinaman nods his head slowly. Oh, the wise pomposity of the Orient!

'Aristarkh Terentich,' the girl calls carelessly, pressing against the smooth leathery shoulder. 'My friend has invited you to keep us company.'

The person fills with animation.

'For reasons beyond the control of the administration . . . out of business,' he whispers, moving his shoulders up and down. 'But I had a past with some stuffing. Truly so. Extremely flattered to make your acquaintance. Sheremetyev.'

Late at night the Chinaman climbed out of the bed and went into the darkness.

'Where're you off to?' Glafira asked hoarsely, her feet kicking.

The Chinaman approached Aristarkh who was snoring on the floor by the sink. He touched the old man's shoulder and threw a meaningful glance at Glafira.

'I say, Vasyuk,' Aristarkh babbled from the floor, 'you're truly obliging.' He ran mincingly towards the bed.

'Go away, you dog,' Glafira said. 'Your Chinaman's murdered me.'

'She's refusing, Vasyuk,' Aristarkh cried hastily. 'You've ordered and she's refusing.

'We friend,' the Chinaman said. 'He may. Eh, bitch . . .'

'You're an oldster,' the girl whispered, making room for the old man, 'and look what notions you have.'

Mikhail Slonimsky (1897–1972)

Slonimsky was born into a highly cultured Jewish family. In 1914 he joined the army as a volunteer and his regiment was one of the first to join the rebellion of 1917. In 1921 he became one of the first members of the literary group Serapion Brothers, and his first collection of stories was published in 1922. Unlike most of his literary friends Slonimsky found little difficulty in complying with the demands of official propaganda, and from the mid-twenties his novels dealt mainly with the problem of converting intellectuals into loyal communists.

The Station Master

A man and a woman approached the station. The man's face looked as if it had been made out of tin: black dust had settled on his sunburnt skin, black stubble bristled on his cheeks and chin. His long nose shone in the sun. His linen trousers had turned the colour of thistles, his canvas blouse was soiled and his yellow shoes were covered in dust.

The woman's clothes had been white once: the blouse, the skirt, the stockings, the shoes. Now it was all green, darkened, tattered. The skin of her face, open neck and forearms was burnt black by the sun.

When the station building, grey like smoke, showed through the foliage, they stopped as if their strength had left them completely. Then they walked on.

The station was protected from the heat of the steppe by the leaves of acacias, elms and maples. Two men jumped out of the garden. One of them, stocky and dark like a Frenchman, ran briskly, his rifle pointing forward, shouting ecstatically, 'Hold it! I'll fire! I swear on my honour I'll fire! Hold it!'

His sweaty face, especially his cheeks and temples, shone. The other man, tall and thin, slowed down so as not to outrun the dark one. His blond hair hung over his forehead, his eyebrows crawled into his eyes, his nose stretched towards his lips and his moustache reached under his chin. The hair, the eyebrows, the nose, the moustache—all were soaked in sweat. His head was bent forward. His rifle was pointed at the sky, but it was more frightening than the dark man's rifle: the tall man's narrow eyes were too indifferent and colourless and there was too much habit in his hands gripping the weapon.

'Not again!' the woman cried.

The man said gloomily, 'All this running for nothing.'

The dark one grabbed the woman by the hand, rolled his eyes in a foreign fashion, then let the woman go and, for some reason, pushed the man. While doing all this he nearly dropped his rifle. He turned to the tall one.

'Milesh, take them to the station.'

Milesh didn't touch the prisoners. He just stepped behind them and the pair moved on as if Milesh had pushed them. The dark one strode in front, his feet turning out in an unnatural way. His blue trousers with a white stripe were tucked into high boots. His wide open white shirt was girdled with a broad green belt. His neck was the same width as the back of his head.

He led the man and the woman through the garden into the station building, stopping in front of a door with a 'Private' notice on it. Unlocking the door, he pushed the prisoners into the room. The key snapped again in the lock.

Someone stood in the room with his back to the window. Blond hair curled over his narrow forehead. His face was a regular oval, his eyes grey, his lips pink.

The man asked him, 'Are you also from the train?'

'No, I'm the station master.'

They fell silent.

The woman looked at them anxiously. Their calm scared her. At last she spoke to the station master: 'What are we going to do?'

He shrugged his shoulders.

'Here is our only weapon.'

He picked up a coiled rope from the bed and threw it on the floor.

'Also these.' He took out of his pocket two rusty nails and held them up.

'I can always hang myself.'

The woman turned pale. Deflated, she swayed and collapsed on the floor.

The man winced.

'I could do without your fainting fits.'

While the station master tried to revive his wife, the man told him about the train crash, the bandits' attack and their escape.

'I knew it was coming,' the station master said. 'They must've broken up the line to the east too. My telegraphist brought the gang here. Last night they killed those who refused to join them. They locked me in here for the time being. This station has a jinx on it. The other day the Whites blew it up, we had to knock up a wooden cover, and now this . . .'

The man looked around the room.

'Excuse me,' he interrupted. 'But I'm dead tired. I expect they're going to shoot us or something of the kind but, to tell you the truth, I don't care any more. I want to sleep.'

He stretched out on the floor and immediately began to snore.

The station master had his own idea of duty. He treated his responsibilities with the seriousness of a man who had in his charge not a small station but a whole country. Now he believed himself responsible for these passengers' lives. He had to save them. When the woman opened her eyes he said, 'Don't worry. I'll think of something.'

The door opened. Milesh came in, handed him a letter in silence and went out, leaving the door open.

The station master opened the letter.

He read:

> 'Dear Nikolai Leontevich, I have decided not to work any more for all those bastards who travel on trains. I have decided to choose an activity which suits me better than the job of a telegraphist at a back-water station. I've put myself at the head of a gang and the world will soon hear of me and my goals. I don't want to kill you. I want you to join me. Here is my offer: in the waiting room, in a corner, my people have put everything necessary to set the station on fire. I've no time to waste. I suggest that you set the station on fire before eight o'clock in the evening. It will be an act which will signal your agreement with me. Moreover, you are to give up protection of the other prisoners. The man and his woman will burn with the station. Until eight o'clock you are free to walk anywhere inside the station, but at any attempt to come out into the garden or onto the platform you will be killed. You will also be killed if you don't carry out my conditions by eight o'clock this evening. I repeat, I don't want to kill you. You're the only person around here who can truly understand me and my goals. But if you don't join me my hand will be firm in killing you.
>
> Sincerely yours, awaiting your response,
> Valerian Blagodatny.'

'What nonsense,' the station master muttered. 'Just look at this!'

He tossed the letter to the woman.

She read it.

Her lips trembled, her brows knitted. She sat up dangling her legs from the bed. She put her left elbow on her knee and propped her cheek on her hand. Her sunburnt face was swarthy like a creole's. Only her eyes were yellow like those of a fox and her hair was the colour of a fox's fur.

'What are you going to do now? You can save yourself. As for the two of us, we're as good as dead.'

'Oh, no!' the station master said with a wry smile. 'If it comes to dying we'll die together.'

He shoved the letter into the pocket of his jacket.

'But it hasn't come to that yet.'

He went out of the room.

The woman jumped to her feet, rushed about the room, shook her husband. He woke up and sat up on the floor, hugging his knees.

'What? What's going on?'

The woman whispered, 'While you slept he wanted to . . . I opened my eyes just in time. Listen, I wasn't asleep, I just pretended to be asleep and I heard them talk. He's in agreement with the bandits. They've decided to set the station on fire and kill you and me. That is, not you and me, but only you. He is planning to take me with him by force. But I'll save you. There's nothing I won't do for your sake. Only believe me and do as I say.'

'The only thing that matters,' her husband interrupted her, 'is whether he's with the bandits.'

'He is.'

'Are you sure?'

'I swear . . . I swear on your life. You can leave me if I am lying. Can't you believe me at a moment like this?'

'Alright. Let's say I believe you.'

'Then this is what you'll do . . .'

While she whispered the station master went to the waiting room. There was straw in a corner. On top of the straw a pile of official papers. A box of matches on the floor. A stroke of a match and his life was saved.

The station master didn't even look at the corner.

He opened the window into the garden and called Blagodatny. The stocky dark man, who had caught the woman and her companion, came out from behind the trees.

'What do you want?' he asked.

'I cannot accept your conditions,' the station master said. 'But I am ready to negotiate.'

'My word is final,' Blagodatny replied. 'I will not retract an iota from my conditions. My letter, as well as my conditions, are the fruit of mature reflection on the life of humankind. Setting the station on fire is an act of abjuration of the false sense of duty. I put my two other prisoners in the same room with you on purpose, as a temptation. A refusal to protect them is a protest against the philistine love which debases a human being. You must rise above those measly philistine sentiments.'

Blagodatny stretched up in order to appear taller, but he was still small.

'In that case,' the station master said. 'You can kill me at eight o'clock in the evening.'

He closed the window and turned away from it. He stopped before the papers piled on the straw. Unable to think of a way out, he stared vacantly at the matchbox.

Suddenly a noose pulled his arms to his body. He struggled, wondering who had thrown a lasso on him as if on a horse. The rope tightened—the rope he had found himself. His legs bent and he fell on the floor. He saw the woman's husband pulling the rope while she stood by giving orders.

'Gag him!'

The station master struggled but the rope was strong. The man stuffed a handkerchief into his mouth.

Trussed up, the station master grew quiet on the floor. He followed the woman with his eyes. She picked up the matchbox, struck a match and put it to the straw. The dry straw caught fire.

The woman turned to her husband.

'Carry him out.'

'But . . .'

'Don't argue with me. You saw that he wanted to set the station on fire and leave you here. He wanted to save me on the pretext of the fire . . . We've no time for talk. Pick him up!'

Blagodatny saw the flames in the waiting room and came up to the porch. He was smiling. He had triumphed over the proud man. He had never doubted he would. A determined will triumphs over everything. He stopped smiling. The couple from the train came out into the garden. The man carried the trussed-up station master. He put the helpless body on the ground. His wife flew to the telegraphist.

'Are you in charge here?'

'I am,' Blagodatny replied.

'I could see it at once in your eyes and . . .'

She blushed.

'He rejected your conditions and we had to tie him up and set the station on fire ourselves.'

'Madam,' the telegraphist said. 'Your actions amaze me. Quite unexpectedly you have proved to be people of exalted thought and adherents of my Idea. You will join me.'

'We are no heroes,' the woman objected. 'We are ordinary people. Please let us go.'

'Madam,' the telegraphist said, 'you have fulfilled the conditions rejected by this pitiful, proud man and my Idea compels me to offer you complete freedom of action. You and your companion are free. Here is your pass.'

He produced a large leather wallet from his pocket and pulled out of it a little green cloth, which he handed to the woman.

She grabbed her husband's hand.

'Let's go!'

The man mumbled as he walked after her, 'I don't understand anything. I don't understand anything at all.'

Beyond the garden a peasant, with a beard as broad as that of a porter, caught up with them. He stood in their way and, looking the woman straight in the eye, said, 'Wicked woman! Ugh, wicked woman! You treacherous fox!'

She shrank, grasping her husband's hand.

The peasant gave her another hard look, spat and walked away.

'What have you done?' her husband asked, although he was beginning to guess what had happened.

She replied curtly, 'Let's go! It's too late to philosophise.'

The station master lay facing the west. In the steppe the setting sun doesn't blind you. It turns cherry-red and sinks quickly. You can look straight at it as it dips into the green land. The sun goes down fast. It touches the ground. The ground is slicing it. Slice after slice. Only a half of the sun remains in the sky, then a quarter, then the ground swallows the sun completely, licking the edge of the sky with a red tongue. The day is finished. It's night.

Blagodatny pulled the handkerchief out of the station master's mouth.

'You're my friend,' he said. 'Although we serve different ideas. It won't be me killing you, it will be one idea killing another.'

He took out his revolver.

'Put away this rubbish,' the station master said calmly. 'And untie me.'

'My word is final,' the telegraphist argued. 'But you have until eight o'clock to repent.'

'Untie me!'

'Do you recant?'

'Untie me!'

'You're good material for my idea of the rebirth of personalities and heroes,' the telegraphist said (-he didn't want to kill this man). 'This idea will fertilise your soul.'

'Untie me,' the station master said again.

Blagodatny ordered, 'Untie him, Milesh!'

Milesh undid the knots and the station master got up, stretching.

Milesh jumped on his horse and galloped off to the place where the wounded still groaned among the carriages scattered on the embankment.

Further delay was dangerous. A punitive force from the town might appear any moment. He had to find out why those men who had attacked the train weren't coming back. Milesh's tall body swung in the saddle like a rifle on the shoulder of a fresh recruit. But this apparent awkwardness had more energy in it than the handsome seat of a true horseman.

Smoke billowed around the station and, rising to the stars, disappeared in the quickly darkening sky. The flames blazed noisily on the roof and walls of the building, shot upwards and sideways, exploded in sparks, and the sparks died. The leaves on the trees dried up and curled. A nearby poplar smouldered. The beams crackled in the fire like a shoot-out.

People watched the fire from behind the trees. There weren't many of them—about twenty—but they had guns in their hands and they were stronger than those without guns, some of whom had escaped while the others had died the night before. Their horses, hobbled but not unsaddled, grazed behind the garden. Blagodatny's horse was tied to a tree apart from the others.

Blagodatny paced up and down the alley, his hands behind his back, his chin on his chest. Ten paces towards the station, ten paces away from the station. He had no grey jacket and cocked hat, and the burning station was nothing like the burning Moscow of a hundred and eight years ago. But this fire was the first of many. Perhaps Moscow would also blaze yet.

A young peasant picked out of the fire a long bamboo cigarette holder with an upturned end. He rolled it on the ground to stop it burning and took it to Blagodatny.

'What's this?' he asked, smiling genially.

Blagodatny didn't even look at him.

The young man asked the station master, 'What's this?'

The station master stood without movement, leaning against the thin trunk of an ash-tree. He turned to the young man.

'It's a cigarette holder,' he said.

'What's a cigarette holder?' the young man asked in amazement.

'It's for smoking,' the station master said. He took the cigarette holder and, for some reason, began to explain in detail how to use it. 'You put this end in your mouth, you understand? You put a cigarette in here. Usually cigarette holders are shorter or the same length as a cigarette, but I used to feel a bit dull at the station on my own, so I got myself this long cigarette holder for amusement. It's my cigarette holder, you see. I used to lie on my bed blowing smoke and imagining I was in Turkey and had a harem and fountains.'

'What's Turkey?' the young man demanded. 'What's a harem?'
'Turkey is a power, a country . . . yes . . . You can have the cigarette holder. Take it. I don't need it any more.'
Their conversation was interrupted by shouts. Milesh had returned with bad news. The main part of the gang, having robbed the train, had taken off to the steppe. Milesh had questioned a dying passenger, who pointed towards the west. The people who had shot him had gone that way. Milesh had finished the passenger off and galloped back to the station. All the loot had gone with the renegades.

People ran to their horses.

Blagodatny ran after them, shouting, 'Hold on! Obey my orders!'

But nobody listened to him.

The young peasant, running past him, brushed him with his elbow. He was holding his cigarette holder in his hand. Blagodatny hit him in the face. The young man stumbled, stopped and, turning to Balgodatny, waved the cigarette holder. Blagodatny snatched the cigarette holder from him and broke it on his knee.

'I'm the boss!' he cried menacingly, his eyes rolling in a foreign fashion. 'I order you to obey me.'

Pointing at the young man, he shouted to Milesh, 'Fire! Shoot him!'

The rifle in Milesh's hands jumped to his shoulder. Its muzzle looked the young man straight in the eye for a moment and he drew back, covering his face with his hands. But the next moment the rifle's muzzle was looking at Blagodatny. Milesh fired and Blagodatny fell, screaming wildly. There was nothing French in him any more. A Russian telegraphist lay on the ground. His eyes didn't roll menacingly. His eyes bulged like those of a fish, staring at Milesh without blinking. Blood trickled from his mouth and, seeing the blood, Blagodatny screamed and wept.

'I'm dying! Save me!'

His scream turned into a rattle.

'Nikolai Leontevich . . . help . . .'

Milesh took aim again.

Blagodatny pressed himself into the ground, shaking in mortal terror.

'Don't . . . I won't do it again . . . don't kill me . . .'

Milesh fired and Blagodatny twitched and grew quiet. His arms were spread, his fingers dug into the ground.

Milesh pointed his rifle at the station master.

But the young peasant stepped between them. His face was pale, he was afraid of Milesh's rifle, while his mouth spoke muddled and convincing words, proving that there was no need to shoot this one.

Milesh slung his rifle over his shoulder and turned to the gang who were waiting for him. The young man, like everybody else, jumped into his saddle and galloped off into the darkness.

The station master was left alone by the burning building. He untied Blagodatny's horse, got into the saddle, and the horse carried him into the steppe.

The ugly red moon was stuck in the sky—not a half-moon or a quarter, but some three-eights, cut off awry. But the stars were strewn in the sky like salt, and that was beautiful. There was no Southern Cross among the stars. The Pole star, a northern Russian star, was in the sky, although the sky over the steppe was a southern sky. It was bluish-black and deep. There was no mist in the steppe.

The station master rode up the hills, trotted down them, galloped between them, past the deep gullies overgrown with thistles. When, at last, he saw the town in the valley he realised how tired he was, as if he had spent the day walking on stilts in the sand.

1923

Nikolai Aseyev (1889–1963)

Aseyev's first book of poetry was published in 1914 and he became one of the leading poets and theoreticians of the left. He nursed a hatred for petty-bourgeois culture so violent that he embraced the Bolshevik Revolution on the grounds that 'it can't be worse'. He survived the vicissitudes of the decades which followed by writing poetry imbued with simple-minded revolutionary romanticism.

The War Against the Rats

The Back Stairs

I live on the ninth floor. It's no height at all for an aeroplane, but for my lungs, harassed by tuberculosis, it is much higher than the Alps. The lift at the back of the house is out of order and, since I can only enter my room from the back stairs, there is plenty of time for thought during the climb to the top. It was during these climbs that I conceived my two-volume classification of the hymenoptera based on the latest discoveries in geology. Apart from that, usually by the time I get to the seventh floor I have finished my next magazine article, sorted out my monthly expenses and solved the chess problem I saw in the morning paper. I like chess because it helps me to make up for wasted time. For instance, one spring while waiting under a dog-rose bush for the birth of a *Papilio machaon* I predicted very accurately, after only ten moves, the end of the game N4 between Lasker and Casablanca in the famous tournament. However, chess is not a passion of mine and I only mention it in order to convey to the reader the complexity of my moves up that staircase. Every climb up those stairs has to be worked out like a game of chess. In the pitiful light of a match (electricity is dead on the back stairs) I have most unexpected encounters. For instance, how am I to understand a single knitted glove with holes in it, which must have been thrown away by one of my neighbours in the face of the approaching spring? A single glove with worn, wide-spread fingers prostrated in a swoon on the sixth stair of the third floor. How am I to understand it, impotently stretched out on the grey concrete in the meagre grey morning light which struggles through the dirty tears of the unwashed windows? It lay there this very morning when I went down the stairs. It became unconsciously imprinted on my mind; in a dusty cobwebbed corner with its dirty yellow colour, its air of hopelessness, its slightly bent fingers. Now, in the measly light of a match, it suddenly rears up and crawls like a crab towards my feet. Or the sudden crash of cans and buckets in the silence of the nocturnal building, exploding unbearably close to me as I gasp and press my trembling hands to my heart which is jumping up and down like a sea-devil. It's them, the grey-yellow agile enemies who crawl in the central heating pipes, bore holes in the wall, float like ghostly silhouettes in the fast-fading glow of a match. Their noise—louder than the tramp of elephants—tears up the thin film of sleep. They jump from the window-sills like brave stuntmen, their fat blind bodies plopping heavily on the floor.

They are disgusting because they make me think of sewers, garbage, squelching yellow mud, the stench and chaos of decay. They also make me think of the future loss of my form, of the seeds of my end surrounding me, of putrefaction and decomposition, of death climbing with impunity up the pipes to me on the ninth floor and tramping wildly in the dark around my bed. They are yellow, impudent gravediggers, storming the highest forms of life, surrounding us with the grey shadows of facelessness and pillage. Our disgust with them comes from a subconscious fear of the cold-blooded, agile impudence of death. The ninth floor stops their progress. If people learned to build houses of nine hundred storeys they would follow us up. Grunting, yelping, coughing, the parasites with their sharks' mouths, their crafty pious faces, would enter, probing the firmness of our walls with their cold paws. Their privilege is not confined to the back stairs. Given half a chance they would crowd the streets and enter the buildings through the front doors, claiming their right to take over everything built by us, everything that yields to their hereditary rodents' teeth, their slippery fat bodies creeping into every opening that is wide enough. But the back stairs are dark, never short of garbage, rusty buckets, coal boxes. Here they can glide, wriggle and dart about. From here they can bore undisturbed into the wood and mortar, and into the hearing of the person climbing upstairs. The winding staircase tightens around the climber like a stone noose. He is pursued by the ghostly ranks of the dirty-grey scouts playing a triumphant march on the rusty cans, dusty empty bottles, and fragments of furniture piled up on the sixth floor landing. The back stairs are my line of retreat before the close enemy columns, which rustle in the dark like a rising tide, undermine the steps of the stairs and hit me under my knees with a surge of deadly terror. A silent grey wave of faces with bared teeth, tramping paws and obstinately arched backs rises like a lump in the throat of the nine-storeyed neurasthenic.

The Other House

The house which I visit more than any other place is stocky, sullen, with a low forehead. It stands on a corner like a criminal caught in the act of changing his clothes—a disorderly, motley fabric of shop signs and windows is pulled over one half of its body. The other half, looking onto a side street, is bare—unwashed yellow skin with a dark bruise of a door. Its lacklustre narrow windows watch the street with sullen menace. A murderer in disguise, it has been stopped dead in its tracks by the searchlight of spring. Its roof bristles like a cheap wig, and animated tresses of smoke escape from under that rusty accessory.

In this house people are stuck together like cold macaroni, swollen in the water that once boiled around them. Sometimes events pierce their solid mass like a fork, pulling them over the edge of their pot. Grey suits are most popular here. Dark frock-coats with buttons up to the chin are also much favoured. The doorbell is answered by the obese host of the fat, flabby cheeks. The tips of his fingers ooze fat, pendants of cut crystal tremble in his beard and his crystal voice jingles out a greeting. One expects a porous rumbling bass. But no. His distinct ringing voice makes one think of the transparent amber fat under the skin of a hefty hog who gives a piercing squeal when kicked with a heavy boot. His wife, with her angular lines of make-up at mouth and eyebrows, lengthens her already long neck with the blackness of silk stretched on strips of bone. A lorgnette and a high hair-slide accentuate even further the narrowness of her shoulders and hips. She is a line drawn across her husband's fatness. As for the guests, some of them are as tall as she, some of them as dry as the furniture and their own conversation. Some of them look like an Englishman just out of hospital. However, there are also fat guests, like sacks of corn. A strange feature common to almost all of them is a raised upper lip and two long front teeth, which creates the impression of a continuous smirk. Amber rolls off the tea-pot spout into the glasses; cookies and marzipans are explored by upper lips, the conversation jumps from the window-sill onto the cornice, from the tea-table onto the hostess' hair, sometimes plopping gently on the floor like a fat chord played on a Bechstein by a long, well-groomed hand.

I come here as an entomologist. I am interested in the similarity between the facial expressions of people and insects. Of course in this house, shining with arrogance and status, you will not find any insects. But the way the people here contract their facial muscles indicates an obscure connection between them and certain kinds of maggots as well as the larva of the cabbage butterfly. For a few evenings I observed the magnified face of a cockroach reminiscing about the glorious life of a landowner. His fixed eyes, the feelers of his moustache and his narrow forehead nearly convinced me that he was invertebrate. But then I had a different idea.

As the noiseless twirling of spoons in tea glasses was drawing to an end, I happened to look down and saw the host fall on all fours and trot under the piano. Unable to believe my eyes, I began to rub them when his head, with a raised upper lip, appeared from under the piano and his sharp voice informed us that the lens from the lorgnette had been found. Otherwise the hostess would have faced three weeks of blindness as such lenses were unobtainable from the local opticians and had to be ordered elsewhere. However, the suspicion stirred by that sudden vision stuck in my subconscious.

They began to talk about the homeless children who prowled the streets in huge numbers, hung in clusters on the tramcars, begged and sometimes stole money from people's pockets.

'They should be cut in four,' a shrill voice piped up from a group of three by the table.

With a start I turned to them and only then realised that they were talking about the pomegranates which the grey suit had offered to the podgy bare back encased in a blueish gown. Just as I concentrated my attention on the pomegranates someone cried from another corner, 'They grow in prisons. That bears a fruit of its own.'

I turned that way and was given a short version of the argument about the homeless children. It was useless to try to divide my attention between two or three topics. By that time the majority of the raised upper lips had been put to the hostess' hand.

The Central Heating and its Labyrinths

The chemist sold me a patent rat poison. For six days they ate it with bread, with cheese rind and with canned beef. They ate it without surprise, without wondering at the generosity of the unexpected treat. I don't think they had particularly sophisticated tastes. But they were quite choosy all the same. For instance, they wouldn't touch potato peel if there was pastry with lard or candied peel. Rat typhus didn't bother them. Even if they had no idea of inoculation their natural immunity was obvious, at least among the troops engaged in the siege of my room. As they grew used to regular evening meals they became more and more demanding at breakfast. Before my very eyes they climbed onto my table if I kept quiet. They must have thought me a conquered patron and they mercifully overlooked the question of reparations in view of my voluntary submission and because of their reluctance to learn the language of the defeated enemy.

However certain conditions, including sleepless nights, were imposed on me without mercy. I decided to defend myself to the end. All the means

I had tried so far had proved ineffective. As my last resort I introduced a
rat trap. It's a simple mechanism: a strong wire frame attached to a spring,
which snaps when the bait is pulled. I put one in every corner, turned off
the light and began to wait.

A distant clink in the iron radiator signalled the approach of their *avant-
garde*. The disgusting yelping of the uninhibited hooligans resounded in
the midnight silence. I waited for a snap and the patter of shadows
scuttling away from a dead relative. But their paws went on thundering
about the dark room, their plops on the floor were as soft as ever, their
yelps piercing, and my revenge slow in coming. I turned on the light and
examined the bait. It had been nibbled at, no more. Their craftiness rose
like an impregnable wall between revenge and my fury.

Three nights passed in fruitless contrivances. I greased the traps with
lard and covered them with food. I kept vigil until morning and still my food
basket was taken apart and my rat traps grew weak under futile strain.

The fourth night found me prostrated before the entrance to their lair.
By an effort of will I shrank to their size. Closing my eyes I groped my way
into the narrow hole, first between crumbling bricks then over rusty iron
which clinked softly under my touch. I reached the iron accordion of the
radiator. The pungent smell of decay filled my nostrils like cotton-wool and
made my head spin. Clenching my teeth I crawled on until I reached their
grey nests, their mouldy bread-crusts, their eyes sparkling in the dark in
irritation and alarm. The bared, sharp blades of their teeth rang like steel
drawn from a scabbard. Their grey whiskers bristled menacingly. They
retreated as I moved towards them. The mossy iron shed a fine rusty
dust, not unlike the fluff on a flower's stamen. I could hear their angry
panting. I managed to drive them out of the central heating into a gap
in the wall. I could not move any further: a solid wall of yellow-green
sparkling eyes shone before me like the lights of a railway terminal. Hair
bristled on their backs, their bared teeth looked like those of wolves. The
rats, pressed against the wall, got ready for attack. The pungent smell of
their sweat was unbearable. Everything became confused in my head. I
lost consciousness.

I was woken up by a repulsive touch. A grey rat with a long tail jumped
off my hand. I raised my head and saw dozens of them running, wriggling,
gliding in the feeble light of dawn. I rose from the floor as their grey herds
galloped around me in a roaring circle. Snatching my coat and hat from
the hook I ran out, jumping down whole flights of stairs. In the street I
didn't recognise myself in a shop mirror. Whilst reading a newspaper in a
cafe, I detached last night's dream from my thoughts like a blood-dripping
bandage. I spent that day in a haze. Towards midday I remembered the

open door of my room and, sufficiently reassured by the noise of the city, went back home. Reaching the seventh floor I heard footsteps descending from my door. Coolly and soberly I raised my head. My acquaintances from the house on the corner, which I visited more than any other place, were coming down the stairs. The greasy host and his tortoise-shell wife walked in front. Then followed almost the entire collection of young grey suits and ladies with splendid spines. Seeing my astonishment they reminded me of the previously agreed trip to the country and of my promise to supply scientific guidance in my capacity as a naturalist. I pleaded insomnia. I must have looked ill enough because they insisted on my going to bed at once. The shuffling of their feet receded downstairs and was cut off by the heavily slammed front door.

The Most Real Thing of All

I tossed and turned in bed until the evening, trying in vain to smooth down my bristling nerves. Sleep was stuck fast somewhere outside my wall. In my delirium I imagined that the silence in my room had disintegrated into a lot of peas which rustled as they rubbed against one another. In the evening I shook myself out of bed like a wilted vegetable. Cold water restored my ability to move normally. I put on my clothes and, unable to bear the silence any more, went out into the spring evening and the quiet honeyed sunset.

The house on the corner stood like an unsolved mystery. A vague memory made me hope that there I would be able to find the missing link in my dream. I rang the doorbell. The familiar maid did not obstruct my legitimate entry, although she did politely try to explain something. I was too preoccupied to pay any attention to her words. Crossing the dark entrance hall I entered the sitting room where people had talked of homeless children and pomegranates. The 'fact that I clearly realised my insanity didn't spare me a start and a fast-beating heart. Round the table, by the piano, in the armchairs, in the corners, their paws crossed on their pink-grey stomachs, sat the grey creatures with round ears and vicious eyes, their upper lips raised over their incisors. Nobody rose as I entered. No chairs moved in the stale, pungent air. A low string inside the piano still moaned, fading away. I understood everything. The typhus took quite a while to act. Those infected all died at the same time. The parasites were silent and the viciousness in their eyes was nothing but the cold vacancy of eyes glazed in death. The samovar boiled dreamily and comfortingly. I tiptoed across the room like a sleep-walking lunatic. Not a single body stirred. Their long tails hung down from the chairs like the banners of a defeated army.

In some room—it must have been mine—an impatient rat trap snapped uselessly. The pressure of the waste gas of thought built up in my head and, as I fell, I felt too lazy to stretch out my hand.

The doctors have ordered complete rest. But they needn't bother warning me against the lethal danger of the slightest movement. What is there to move for when I am convinced, beyond doubt, that all my spectral enemies are dead? I know for sure of the destruction of their lair, of the death of their cunning and impudence. I am the one responsible for their defeat. In the neat and peaceful white house where I am resting now there is absolutely nothing they can do. As for the outside, I have designed a clever mechanism which is bound to overcome their suspicion and craft. My sleep is forged of iron links which no teeth can gnaw apart.

1923

Mikhail Zoshchenko (1885–1958)

Zoshchenko was the son of a Ukrainian painter and an actress. He studied law but did not graduate. In 1914 he volunteered for the army, and after the Revolution wandered about the country from job to job; tormented by persistent depression, he tried on several occasions to commit suicide. He published his first book of comic stories in 1921 and soon became the most popular writer in Russia. He later undertook a programme of self-analysis, which he described in the book *Before Sunrise*, for which he was reviled and persecuted by the authorities, and, from 1946, forced into silence.

The Gentlewoman

I, brothers, don't like women who wear hats. If you give me a woman in a hat, even if she wears silk stockings or a dog, or a gold tooth, this gentlewoman to me is not a woman at all but an empty vessel.

I must say, in my time, when I was superintendant of a block of flats, I did get involved with a gentlewoman. I went out with her and took her to the opera. The whole thing happened at the opera. At the opera she demonstrated her ideology in its entire form.

I met her in our block of flats. At a meeting. I see a kind of lady standing there wearing stockings and a gold tooth.

'Where are you from, citizen?' I ask, 'From which apartment?'

'I'm from number seven,' she says.

'That's alright,' I say, 'Go on living there.'

I liked her very much from the start. I began to visit her often. At number seven. I used to visit her in my official capacity. 'How are things with you, citizen, in the sense of running water and sewage? Is it in order?'

'Yes,' she says, 'it's in order.'

She would wrap herself in her shawl and there wouldn't be another squeak out of her. Only the eyes were looking. And the tooth in her mouth shining. I visited her thus for a month and she got used to me. She began to answer me in detail. 'Yes, the pipes are alright, thanks to you, Grigori Ivanovich.'

Eventually I began taking her for walks in the street. When we came out she ordered me to take her arm. I would take her arm and drag myself after her like a pike out of water. I didn't know what to say to her and I felt ashamed in front of people.

Once she said to me, 'Why do you lead me up and down the street all the time? It makes me dizzy. As you are my escort and an official, why don't you take me to the opera, for example?'

'It can be done,' I say.

Fortunately the Party organiser was distributing opera tickets at the time. I got one ticket. Vaska the plumber gave me another one.

I didn't look at the tickets, but later it turned out that they were not together, one in the circle, the other in the gods.

Well, we went. Sat down at the opera. She sat on my seat and I sat on Vaska's. I was at the very top and I couldn't see a bloody thing. However if I bent over the rail I could see her. Not very well though. I endured boredom for a while, then I went downstairs. It was the interval by then. She was walking around.

'Hullo,' I say.

'Hullo.'

'I wonder,' I say, 'if the sewage is in order here.'

'I don't know,' she says.

Meanwhile she goes to the buffet. I go after her. She looks at the cakes. I grovel at her feet like a wretched capitalist and suggest, 'If you feel like eating a piece of cake, have it. I am paying.'

'Merci,' she says.

She went up to the cakes in a debauched manner, grabbed a piece with cream on it and began to gobble it.

My funds were rather low then. The most I could pay for was three pieces of cake. While she ate, I anxiously fingered the money in my pocket, trying to feel with my hand how much I had. It wasn't much.

She finished one piece and grabbed another. I grunted. But I couldn't speak. A kind of bourgeois shame came over me. What kind of an escort was I, without funds?

I walked around her like a rooster while she laughed and fished for compliments. I say, 'Isn't it time we went back to our seats? It seems the bell has rung.'

She says, 'No.' And takes another piece of cake.

I say, 'Isn't it too much on an empty stomach? It may make you sick.'

'No,' she says, 'I am used to it.' And takes another piece of cake.

At that point the blood went to my head.

'Put it back!' I say.

That scared her. She opened her mouth and the tooth shone in it. I lost control of myself. 'To hell with it,' I think, 'I'm not going out with her again anyway.'

'Put that bloody cake back!' I say.

She puts it back. I say to the waiter, 'How much do we owe you for three pieces of cake?'

The waiter pretends indifference, playing the fool.

'For four pieces of cake,' he says, 'you owe me such and such a sum.'

'How can it be four,' I say, 'when the fourth piece is on the plate?'

'No,' he says, 'Although it is on the plate, it has a bite taken out of it and an indentation made with a finger.'

'What indentation?' I say, 'For Christ's sake. It's only your peculiar fantasy.'

A crowd gathered, of course. Experts. Some say there is a bite, others—there isn't.

I turned my pockets out and, of course, all sorts of rubbish fell to the floor. People laugh. I don't feel like laughing. I count my money. It turns out I had exactly the price of four pieces of cake. All that riot was for nothing.

I paid the money and said to the lady, 'Finish your piece of cake, citizen. It's been paid for.'

But she didn't move. She was ashamed to finish the cake. Then a gentleman interfered.

'Let me finish it,' he said.

He finished it, the bastard. On my money.

When we got home she said in her bourgeois tone of voice, 'I've had enough of this impertinence. If you don't have money, don't take ladies to the opera.'

I said, 'Money is not the only thing in the world, if you'll pardon the expression.'

We parted at that.

No, I don't like gentlewomen.

1923

Steam Baths

They say, citizens, steam baths in America are excellent.

There, for example, a citizen comes, throws his clothes into a special box and goes to wash. He doesn't even worry, say, about theft or disappearance, he doesn't even take a ticket. Well, perhaps some nervous American may say to the attendant, 'Good-bye,' he might say, 'Would you keep an eye on my clothes?' That's all.

This American washes, comes back, and they give him his clothes clean—washed and pressed. The leggings are whiter than snow. Underpants mended, patched. The good life!

Our steam baths aren't bad either. But worse. Still you can wash in them. Only with us there is the trouble with tickets. Last Saturday I went to the steam baths (being unable to go to America)—they gave me two tickets. One for underwear, the other for my coat and hat.

But where can a naked man put tickets? I'll tell you straight—nowhere. There are no pockets. Nothing but stomach and legs. These tickets are nothing but trouble. You can't tie them to your beard.

Well, I tied a ticket to each leg, so I wouldn't lose them both together. I entered the baths.

Now the tickets are flapping against my legs. Walking is a bore. But I have to walk. Because I need a wash bowl. What is washing without a wash bowl? Nothing but trouble.

I am looking for a wash bowl. I see one citizen washing himself in three wash bowls. He's standing in one, soaping his head in another and holding the third one with his left hand so nobody can steal it.

I tugged at the third wash bowl. I wanted to take it for myself, you know, but the citizen held on.

'What do you think you're doing,' he says, 'stealing other people's wash bowls? I'll hit you,' he says, 'between the eyes with this wash bowl—you won't be pleased.'

I say, 'It's not,' I say, 'the Tsarist regime, we don't hit people with washing bowls. What egotism,' I say. 'Other people have to wash too. We are not in the theatre,' I say.

He turns his back to me and goes on washing.

'I can't stand here breathing down his neck,' I think. 'Now he'll keep washing for three days on purpose.'

I walked away.

In an hour I see a man who's off his guard, he has let go of his washing bowl. Either he bent over to pick up his soap or was lost in a daydream, I don't know. But I took that washing bowl for myself.

Now I have a washing bowl, but there's nowhere to sit down. And what is washing when you have to stand? Nothing but trouble.

Well, I stand, hold the washing bowl in my hand, wash. All around, God Almighty, laundering goes on at full swing. One man is washing his trousers, another rubbing his underpants, a third wringing something else—no sooner had I washed than I was dirty again. They are slopping dirty water all over, the devils. And the noise that went on with this laundering! I didn't feel like washing. I couldn't hear where I rubbed my soap. Nothing but trouble.

To hell with them, I think. I'll finish washing at home.

I go to the dressing room. They give me my clothes for my ticket. I look—everything is mine, the trousers aren't mine.

'Citizens,' I say, 'my trousers had a hole here. And these have it in another place.'

The attendant says, 'We're not here to guard your holes. We are not in the theatre,' he says.

Well, I put the trousers on, go to collect my coat. They don't give me my coat, a ticket is required. And I forgot the ticket on my leg. I have to undress. I take my trousers off, look for the ticket—no ticket. The string is there, on my leg, but the ticket is gone. The paper got washed off.

I give the string to the attendant—he doesn't want it.

'I don't give coats in exchange for string,' he says. 'Any citizen can cut lots of strings—there won't be enough coats. Wait,' he says, 'till everybody leaves—I'll give you what's left.'

I say, 'Brother, what if some rubbish is left? We are not in the theatre,' I say. 'I'll tell you what it looks like. One pocket is torn, the other missing. As for the buttons, the top one is there, the lower ones are past hoping for.'

He gave it to me in the end. And he didn't take the string. I put my coat on and went out. Suddenly I remembered—I left my soap behind.

I went back again. They wouldn't let me in in my coat.

'Take it off,' they say.

I say, 'I can't undress for the third time, citizens. We are not in the theatre,' I say. 'At least give me the price of my soap.'

They don't.

They can have it. I went home without the soap.

Of course you may wonder, which steam baths were they? Where are they? What's the address?

Which steam baths? Any ordinary ones. The ones where you pay ten kopeks.

1924

The Actor

This story is about a real event. It happened in Astrakhan. An amateur actor told it to me.

This is what he told me:

You are asking me, citizens, whether I was an actor? Well, I was. I played in the theatre. I came into contact with this art. It's all nonsense. There's nothing extraordinary about it . . .

Of course, if you think more deeply about it, this art has a lot of good in it.

Say, you come on the stage, and the audience are watching. Among the audience there are friends, relatives on your wife's side, citizens from your apartment house. They are winking at you from the stalls—come on, Vasya, do your best. And you make signs at them—don't you worry, citizens, I know, I wasn't born yesterday.

But if you think still deeper, there's nothing good in this profession. It makes more bad blood than it's worth.

Once we produced a play, 'Who is to Blame?' From the old days. It's a very powerful play. In it, in one act, robbers rob a merchant before the eyes of the audience. It comes out very naturally. The merchant screams, kicks at them. And they rob him. A terrifying play.

So we produced this play.

Right before the performance the amateur who played the merchant had a few drinks. In the heat he got so drunk that we saw he couldn't carry on with the merchant's part. When he approached the limelights he smashed the bulbs with his foot on purpose.

The producer, Ivan Palych, says to me, 'We can't let him on in the second act. The son of a bitch will smash all our bulbs. Maybe you'd play in his place? The audience is stupid, they won't see the difference.'

I say, 'I can't go before the limelights, citizen. Don't ask me. I've just eaten two water melons. My thinking isn't clear.'

But he says, 'Help us out, brother. Just for one act. Maybe in the meantime that actor will sober up. Don't disrupt our educational work,' he says.

They prevailed upon me. I went before the limelights.

According to the play I came on just as I was, in my jacket and trousers. I just stuck on someone else's beard. And came on.

The audience, although stupid, recognised me at once.

'Ah,' they say, 'Vasya has come on! Don't be afraid, do your best . . .'

I say, 'There's no time for being afraid, citizens,' I say, 'as it is a critical moment. The artiste,' I say, 'is under the influence and can't come before the limelights. He's throwing up.'

We began to act.

I am playing the merchant. I scream, kick at the robbers. And I feel that one of the amateurs indeed has put his hand in my pocket. I wrapped my jacket around me and moved away from the artistes. I try to beat them off. I hit them right in their faces. By God, I do!

'Don't come near me,' I say, 'you bastards, I'm telling you straight.'

But they, according to the play, close in on me. They took out my wallet, (180 roubles), and reached for my watch.

I scream in a terrible voice, 'Help, citizens, they are robbing me for real.'

This only produced a completely realistic effect. The stupid audience clapped in delight. They shout, 'Come on, Vasya, come on. Beat them off, man. Hit the devils over the heads.'

I scream, 'It's no use, brothers!'

Meanwhile I am hitting them right over their heads.

I see one of the amateurs bleeding while the others, the bastards, are getting excited and keep pressing me.

'Brothers,' I scream, 'What's this? What am I suffering for?'

The producer stuck his head out from behind the curtain.

'Atta boy,' he says. 'Your acting is great, Vasya. Carry on.'

I can see my screams are no help. Because whatever I scream it all fits into the play.

I fell to my knees.

'Brothers,' I say, 'Producer Ivan Palych,' I say, 'I can't go on. Bring down the curtain. My last savings are being stolen from me for real!'

Then some of the theatre experts saw that the words weren't in the play. They came out from the wings. The prompter, thank God, crawled out of his hole.

'Citizens,' he says, 'it looks like they've really stolen the merchant's wallet.'

They brought the curtain down. A ladle full of water was brought and they gave me a drink.

'Brothers,' I say, 'Producer Ivan Palych, what's this?' I say. 'In the course of the play someone took my wallet.'

Well, they frisked the amateurs. They didn't find my money. My empty wallet was thrown into the wings.

The money was gone. As if burned.

Art, you say? I know! I acted!

1925

Cine-drama

I have nothing against the theatre. But the cinema is better still. It's more economical than the theatre. For example, you don't have to take your coat off—that saves you pennies every time. Also there's no need to shave—nobody will see your face in the dark.

The only bad thing is getting into a cinema. It's quite difficult to enter. They can easily crush you to death.

As for the rest, it's quite decent. Viewing is easy.

On my wife's birthday she and I went to see a cine-drama. We bought tickets. We began to wait.

Quite a few people gathered. They all hovered in front of the door.

Suddenly the door opened and a lady said, 'Push in.'

At once a little crush began. Because everybody wants to get an interesting seat.

People rushed at the door. They created a bottle-neck at the door.

The ones behind push and the ones in front can't go anywhere.

I was suddenly squeezed like a sardine and carried to the right.

'Oh dear,' I think. 'I don't want to smash the door.'

'Citizens,' I scream. 'Easy, for God's sake! You're smashing the door with a man.'

By then quite a stream had formed, pushing like mad.

A military man was pushing me from behind in a very uncultured way. The son of a bitch was practically drilling my back.

I kicked this military devil with my foot.

'You, citizen,' I say, 'leave off your dirty tricks.'

Suddenly I was lifted slightly and my face hit the door.

So, I think, they've taken to smashing doors with cinema-goers.

I wanted to pull away from that door. I began to hammer my way through with my head. They wouldn't let me. Then I saw that my trousers had got hooked on the door handle. My pocket.

'Citizens,' I cry, 'take it easy, help! A man is hooked on the door handle.'

They cry back at me, 'Get unhooked, comrade! Those at the back have rights too.'

How can I get unhooked when they're pulling like hell and there's no way to lift a finger?

'Stop it,' I scream, 'you devils! Stop taking my trousers off me. Let a man off the handle first. The cloth is ripping.'

Do they hear? They are pushing . . .

'Lady', I say, 'at least you could look away, for God's sake. I am being pulled out of my trousers against my will.'

But the lady had turned blue and was rattling. She wasn't interested in looking at me.

Suddenly, thank God, I was borne away.

I think, either I've got unhooked or they've taken me out of my trousers.

The crush had eased by then.

I took a freer breath and looked at myself. The trousers were there. One leg had been ripped in two and was flapping like a sail when I walked.

That's how they undress the viewers, I think.

In this state I went to look for my wife. She had been squashed into the orchestra. She was sitting there, afraid to come out.

Then, thank God, they turned the lights off. They started the film.

It's hard for me to tell you what kind of film it was; I spent the whole time pinning my trousers together.

Fortunately my wife had a pin. Also some kind-hearted woman took four pins out of her underwear. I also found a piece of string on the floor.

I tied and pinned my trousers together and by that time the drama was over—thank God. Then we went home.

1926

The Case History

To tell you the truth I prefer to be ill at home. Of course, it goes without saying, in a hospital you get more light and more culture. And the calorific content of food is more calculated there. Still, at home, as they say, even straw is food.

They brought me to hospital with typhoid fever. My relatives thought in that way they'd relieve my incredible suffering.

But they failed to achieve their purpose because it happened to be a hospital where nothing was to my liking.

They bring a patient there and write down his name in a book while he reads a notice on the wall—'Corpses are issued to relatives from 3 to 4 p.m.'

I don't know about other patients but as for me, I literally swayed on my feet when I read that announcement. The thing is that I am running a high temperature, life is hardly flickering in my organism, you could easily say it is hanging by a thread—I am in no state to read such words.

I said to the man who was writing down my name, 'Why do you display such indecent notices, comrade medical attendant? Don't you know that the patients are not interested in reading such things?'

My saying this surprised the medical attendant and he replied, 'Look at him. He's so ill he can hardly walk. He's got such fever that his breath is steaming. And he criticises everything. If you recover, which is unlikely, then criticise to your heart's content. Otherwise we'll issue you from 3 to 4 p.m. in the form indicated here, then you'll know.'

I wanted to grapple with this medical attendant, but as my temperature was running over 110, I gave up arguing with him. I only said to him, 'You just wait, you medical catheter. When I recover you'll answer to me for your impudence. Do you think it does the patients any good to listen to such speeches? It saps their strength, that's what it does.'

The medical attendant was surprised to hear a seriously ill patient speak so freely, so he shut up. Then a nurse came running. 'Come along,' she says, 'to the washing station.'

These words made me wince. 'I wish you'd call it bathroom,' I say, 'instead of washing station. It's a prettier word and it ennobles a patient. I am not a horse to be taken to a washing station.'

The nurse says, 'In spite of being ill he notices all sorts of subtleties. Judging by his propensity for meddling, I don't think he'll ever recover.'

She brought me to the bathroom and told me to take off my clothes. Just as I began to undress I noticed that in the bathtub there was a head sticking out of the water. On closer inspection I saw an old lady sitting in the bath, apparently one of the patients.

I say to the nurse, 'Where have you brought me, you devils—to the ladies' bathroom? Someone is already bathing here.'

The nurse says, 'It's just a sick old woman sitting there. Pay no attention to her. She's running a high temperature and she doesn't react to anything. So take off your clothes and don't be embarrassed. Meanwhile we'll take the old woman out of the tub and draw you some fresh water.'

I say, 'The old woman doesn't react but I still do. I find it positively unpleasant to see what you've got swimming in your tub.'

The medical attendant appeared again.

'It's the first time,' he says, 'that I've seen such a squeamish patient. He never stops complaining. He even has the impudence to complain about a dying old woman taking a bath. Maybe she has a temperature over 110 and doesn't react to anything. Maybe she sees everything like through a sieve. I can tell you one thing for sure, the sight of you won't keep her in this world another five minutes. No, I much prefer unconscious patients. At least they find everything to their liking and don't engage us in any scientific arguments.'

At this point the bathing old woman piped up, 'Take me out of the water,' she said, 'or I'll get out myself and give you hell.'

They got busy with the old woman and told me to take my clothes off. Knowing my character they stopped arguing with me and agreed with everything I said.

They put me in a smallish room which contained about thirty patients with various kinds of diseases. Some of them were seriously ill. Others, on the contrary, were recovering. Some of them whistled. Others played chequers. Still others shuffled from room to room spelling out various notices on the walls.

I said to the nurse, 'If this is a nut-house, you just tell me so straight. I've been in many hospitals but I've never seen anything like this. In other hospitals there is silence and order and you've got a regular bazaar here.'

She said, 'Maybe you want us to put you in a private room with a sentry to keep flies and fleas away?'

I screamed for the doctor but the same medical attendant came. Well, I was in a frail state. When I saw him I passed out completely.

I came to, I think, after three days.

The nurse says to me, 'You've got an iron constitution. We put you near an open window, by mistake, and even so you've recovered. Now, if you don't catch anything from the other patients, you can be congratulated on your recovery.'

However, when it came to discharging me, after all I had been through, I developed a nervous complaint. From nerves I broke out in a rash. The doctor said, 'Stop being nervous and it will soon pass.'

I was nervous because they wouldn't discharge me. The medical attendant said, 'We are so overworked that we have no time to discharge patients. You're a fine one to complain, you've only overstayed eight days. Some patients have been waiting three weeks, they don't complain.' Eventually they discharged me and I came home.

My wife said, 'You know, Peter, a week ago we thought you had kicked the bucket because we received a letter from the hospital saying, "On receiving this letter come at once to the hospital and take away your husband's body."'

My wife had gone to the hospital and they had apologised for their clerical error. Someone else had died and they thought for some reason it was me, while by that time I had recovered except for the nervous rash. That incident gave me an unpleasant taste and I wanted to go back to the hospital and have another row. But when I remembered what went on there I thought better of it.

Now when I am ill I stay at home.

1936

Alexander Grin
(1880–1932)

Grin joined the Socialist Revolutionary Party in the early 1900s and discovered his literary talent whilst writing political pamphlets. *The Cripple* is not typical of his work, most of which is characterised by an exotic romanticism. Grin's work was received with indifference by the official critics and he died in poverty and obscurity.

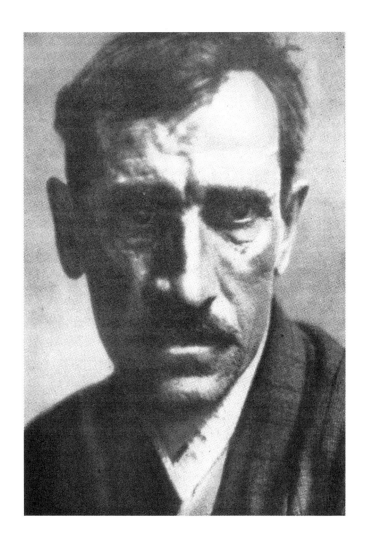

The Cripple

As a rule I dislike mirrors. They lend a ghost-like quality to everything that happens behind one's back, an impression of an immobile wall of water, a frozen vista with no end and no objects in its depth.

Especially weird are reflections in street mirrors with their vertical distortions, where walls rear up and lean over you and the street slopes away like a ship-deck in a storm, so that you can't help looking away.

Usually we look at ourselves from inside without dissociating our vaguely-remembered appearance from our thoughts and feelings. That's why we tend to be on the defensive whenever we see that living form—our face—abstracted from us into a defenceless condition.

I would never have turned to that mirror with its dumb prompting had it not been for a remark made in an undertone.

'Look, a cripple. Give him something.'

The speaker was a woman. They are more compassionate than men, perhaps because they have a livelier emotional, as opposed to visual, imagination.

Turning round I saw a man in a tattered overcoat squatting on his haunches in a little box on wheels. He had a swollen young face with a lifeless complexion. All life in this captive, who had been cut in half, was concentrated in his shining eyes, which scanned intently the faces in the crowd moving above him. All the violently arrested mobility of his body was expressed in that look which darted about like an animal on a leash. His shoulders were hunched forward, his hands leaned against the edge of his box, his crutches lay on the ground nearby.

Sometimes, raising his black hat and tightly pulling it on again, he gave me an impression of grotesque well-being so that, with a slight effort, I could imagine that he was half-hidden in the ground, like a digger in a ditch, and that he had legs.

What kept me near him was a desire to overcome myself, to comprehend his sensations, his constant feeling of shortness, his distorted heart-beat, the peculiar course of his thoughts, always associated with his condition.

I don't know why I bothered as I cannot stand cripples. I have a grumpy resistance to these altered, sewn-up bodies which bring ugly sorrow into one's fresh and peaceful world. We look for harmony even in rags, for the picturesque in a smoke-filled attic. The sight of courageous poverty moves us more than a simple, hungry wail, because the former's picturesqueness stimulates our imagination.

Whenever I see a cripple I become cold, curious and detached.

That was exactly how I felt now as, not wishing to embarrass the poor wretch, I studied his reflection in the mirror. I noticed that he stared back at me, perhaps expecting a hand-out.

It must have been on his mind.

I am convinced that he looked at every passer-by with the same thought in mind and that his indignation must have been continuous because scarcely one out of a hundred gave him anything. When they did he bowed mechanically, and his bright eyes resumed the search in silence. He obviously considered wailing and chattering superfluous.

When a few notes had accumulated in his box he unhurriedly sorted them out and distributed them among his pockets, looking straight in front of him with the absentminded air of a book-keeper.

Although I understood that the air of professional unconcern was a cover for his inner turmoil, in my unwitting cynicism I thought him a bit too histrionic.

The cripple was repugnant to me but I couldn't turn away from the mirror. I scrutinised him avidly, imagining around him fragmentary pictures of battle, exploding shells, a grey morning with a pink stripe where medical orderlies stumbled in the dark under the weight of stretchers. The groaning on the battlefield, monotonous like the singing of a samovar, mingled with a distant cannonade.

Then surgery, awakening to a new, difficult life, a thousand small devices never before heard of, dreams of legs, a new concept of oneself, years of despair and dark indifference.

Meanwhile I became aware that, in my nervous, impressionable state of mind, my hands were moving mechanically in imitation of the cripple's movements as he shuffled his money and changed his position in the box. My abrupt incomplete movements irritated me in the extreme and I began to look at other people both in the mirror and on the pavement.

The countless movements of legs, the pulsation of a multitude of women's ankles, the galoshes, shoes and felt boots taking measured bites out of the pavement, the noise, the rattle, the shuffle and the rustle of the moving crowd reminded me pleasantly of the strength and balance which enabled me to walk the entire length of Tverskaya Street uphill as wall as downhill.

The cripple in his box must have had a different idea of space. To him it must have been almost a fiction, a forgotten dream. The nearest corner must require the complex calculation suited to a huge distance. The roof of the Gnezdikovsky tower-block must have seemed to him as high as Mont Blanc.

Here my thoughts suddenly lit up and darted after a woman who had passed hurriedly behind my back. I recognised her at once and recalled what had happened seven months before.

I saw myself climbing a staircase to the fourth floor where the door was opened by two sisters who were familiar with the way I rang the bell. The younger one, her arm round her sister's waist, demanded quizzically, 'Well?' The elder sister gave me a shy smile. Her shyness was welcoming. I felt shy myself and it pleased me.

What had parted us? I couldn't remember. I have a terrible memory. My first impulse was to run after her, but for some reason, when she was within two paces, I didn't. Then I found myself unable to move.

I seemed to have turned to stone. I just stood there trying to understand something but my thoughts were in disorder. My pale reflection in the mirror and the bright original, in the street reflected behind my back, became confused and a terrible realisation took my breath away.

Yes, I was looking at myself, having forgotten what had happened to me. I had no legs, my crutches lay nearby on the ground, and the passers-by looked down at me, throwing me the odd banknote.

Indeed it was like an awakening. Mirrors cause dreams, a strange mixture of past and present, a distortion of outlook, aims and impressions. That whirl had vanished. The reality of the day, the multitudes of strangers' legs passing, pierced me painfully, nailing me to my box, leaving me to grope round my stumps and to shuffle my banknotes. Why do I always look at legs and think about legs?

Where are my legs which took me to the fourth floor so that I might feel shy and look into her eyes? I looked away from the mirror.

With a sob and a bitter howl, triumphant in the impunity of a legless lost man who had been cut in two, I picked up my crutches.

The damn mirror! I smashed it—wham! The fragments of glass glittered sharply against the exposed wood. The whole thing was the funniest sight I ever saw.

But I didn't care any more. I didn't care.

1924

Ilya Ilf & Evgeny Petrov
(1897–1937; 1903–1942)

Their real names were Ilya Fainzilberg and Evgeny Kataev, and although both were born in the Jewish Odessa they only met in 1925, in Moscow, while on the staff of the railwaymen's magazine 'Whistle'. They wrote their first novel, *The 12 Chairs*, in 1928. It was a tremendous success and in 1931 they produced a sequel, *The Golden Calf*. Both novels were among the most popular ever to have been written in Russia. After Ilf's death of tuberculosis, Petrov wrote nothing of significance; he was killed in a plane crash while working as a war correspondent in 1942.

The Idealist Nikudykin

Vasya Nikudykin struck his hollow chest with his fist and said, 'To hell with our shame which prevents us from establishing a true equality between the sexes! Down with trousers and skirts! To hell with the rags covering the most beautiful, the most graceful thing in the world, the human body! We'll go out into the streets and squares without these ignominious clothes! We'll stop the passers-by and say to them, "Passers-by, you must follow our example! You must undress! To hell with shame!" Hurrah!'

'You can't mean that, Nikudykin. You're not going anywhere. You, Nikudykin, will never take off your trousers,' said one of his admirers.

'Who, I? I'll never take off my trousers?' Nikudykin demanded with a somewhat abating fervour.

'You won't. You'll never take off your trousers.'

'I'll never go out naked?'

'You'll never go out naked.'

Nikudykin turned pale but there was no retreat.

'I will,' he muttered cheerlessly. 'I'm going.'

Sighing heavily and covering a large boil on his side with his hand, Nikudykin went out.

A thin, prickly rain was falling.

Writhing in the cold, Nikudykin waddled downtown on his bent, hairy legs. The passers-by, casting suspicious sidelong glances at the hunched-up lilac figure, hurried on to their destinations.

'Never mind,' Nikudykin thought bravely, his teeth chattering. 'N . . . n . . . never mind. 'You just wait till I get on a tram and give a demonstration. Then you'll take notice of me, you wretched little people in trousers!'

Nikudykin got on a tram.

'Your fare, citizen,' the strict conductor said.

Nikudykin automatically put his hand where people usually have a pocket, but found only his boil. 'I'll demonstrate,' he thought.

'Down with these trousers and skirts!' he mumbled.

'Citizen, you're holding up the tram! Get off!'

'Down with the rags covering the most beautiful thing in the world, the human body!' Nikudykin insisted.

'What the hell is going on here!' the passengers railed. 'Either pay your fare or get off!'

The people are blind, Nikudykin thought, retreating towards the exit. They don't even notice I'm naked.

'I'm naked and I'm proud of it,' he said with a wry smile.

'This is outrageous!' the passengers cried. 'The fellow's been keeping the tram waiting for five minutes. Conductor, do something!'

The conductor did something.

Nikudykin found himself on the pavement. Rubbing his aching knee he limped towards Theatre Square.

What I need now is a big demonstration, he thought. I'll stand in the middle of the square and give a speech. Or I'll stop a passer-by and say to him, 'Passer-by, take off your clothes.'

Nikudykin's skin, which during his journey had changed through all the colours of the rainbow, looked like a livid, shagreen leather briefcase. His lower jaw was doing a tap dance in the cold. His arms and legs were cramped.

Nikudykin grabbed a passer-by by the skirt of his coat.

'P . . . p . . . passer-by . . . yyyyy . . . down . . . vvvvv . . . with your trousers . . . vvvvv.'

The passer-by hurriedly put a shining new coin in Nikudykin's hand and said sternly, 'Young man, instead of twiddling your thumbs you ought to find yourself a job, you know. Then you'll have trousers.'

'But I'm naked on principle,' Nikudykin said with a sob. 'I'm naked . . . You too must be naked, citizen . . . Don't conceal your beauty.'

'Find yourself a job, my dear chap. Then you won't be naked any more,' the passer-by moralised.

Nikudykin looked at the coin in his hand and burst into tears.

He spent the night in a police station.

1924

Gus and the Stolen Planks

Ksavery Gus possessed two unquestionable and universally admired qualities: a massive red nose and an equally massive erudition. The former was inexplicable. The latter had been acquired at a faculty of law. Before the Revolution he had been a barrister's secretary. He hardly ever refered to his former grandeur, preferring to enjoy his grandeur of the moment. His job with the Criminal Investigation Department didn't prevent him from singing in a baritone, (definitely a baritone), 'Two grenadiers to France . . .' to my accompaniment in our modest village theatre.

At the time I worked for the local news agency. I worked honestly and with zeal, dashing from town to town in search of hot news. Those days were full of hardship which made them three times as exciting, and I managed in the course of one day to visit two opposite ends of the district. In the imperturbable German settlements I roared leading articles from club stages, (we delivered regular spoken newspapers). In the slovenly Ukrainian villages I hectically recorded news for various district congresses. In the steppe hamlets I fought packs of wild dogs. Then sitting in a cart, which dived now into the yellow wheat, now into a jungle of corn, I wrote poems under the blue Ukrainian sky. Everything was fine until that meeting. That meeting brought me low.

I met him at the People's House. I was sitting at the piano. Next to me sat a girl. She was blonde and, in spare time from her pedagogical activities at the local school, she had conquered my honest pressman's heart shortly before that momentous day. Ksavery Gus entered the room in the company of a policeman and, looking my blonde up and down, whispered to his satellite, 'She isn't bad, that blonde.'

Then he looked me straight in the eye and said, 'Now let's see your papers.'

Despite the July heat and the impressive-looking document in my pocket, I broke out in a cold sweat.

'What's the matter, comrade? Who are you?'

'Who am I? I like that,' he said, eyeing my girl. 'I'm the head of the Criminal Investigation Department. Now let's see your papers or I'll have to arrest you.'

He read my document.

'I'm sorry. A minor misunderstanding. My fault. Anyway, glad to meet you.' He put out his hand. 'Gus. Ksavery. This is officer Bufalov. Go back to the department, Bufalov. Tel Pertsman I won't be long.'

He introduced himself to my blonde and, draping himself artistically over the piano, began to speak. He started with music and ended with a sad story of the theft of two bay mares. In between he informed us that he had a wife who was a pianist and a brother who was secretary of the district revolutionary tribunal.

By the evening we had become friends. We walked up and down the main street and talked, talked, talked. For four hours words like recidivist, burglar, murderer, bandit were mentioned in both plural and singular in every possible declension. I was overwhelmed by my new friend's greatness. He offered me a job with the Criminal Investigation Department. I couldn't make a decision. He reproached me. He painted seductive pictures. He showed me his gun. I gave in.

For the first time in two weeks, lying in bed I didn't think of my blonde. I thought of my future career. I had a terrible dream. I lay in ambush, a gun in my hand, waiting for a bandit. He came. I shouted, 'Hands up!' Paying no attention to me he kept walking. I pulled the trigger and my gun misfired. I pulled the trigger again, and again my gun misfired. I pulled the trigger for a third time and still my gun misfired. The bandit was coming straight towards me. A bomb glistened in his hand. I woke up in a cold sweat. The sun was rising. The cocks were crowing.

At ten o'clock in the morning I entered the police station. The duty officer, pointed at the door with a plaque on it saying, 'Head of the Criminal Investigation Department. Do not enter unannounced.' I was impressed. I asked the duty officer to announce me. Refusing to oblige, he kicked the door open and told me to go right in.

In a smallish room with a wooden floor and peeling wallpaper there stood a large desk. At the desk sat Gus and a huge man I didn't know, who was glueing together large sheets of paper covered with figures. What resulted was a kind of tablecloth which he hung carefully on the backs of the chairs. I was young and naive then and I didn't know that the tablecloth was nothing but the Department's monthly report.

Gus greeted me with dignity.

'Good morning. May I introduce my colleague Pertsman. Pertsman, this is our new officer.'

'Do you know how to keep a register?' Pertsman boomed.

The question threw me a bit. I mumbled something about fighting bandits.

'Who cares about bandits when almost every day we have to send in some kind of report?'

Pertsman spat viciously and resumed his glueing.

'Be quiet, Yasha. Don't confuse him. I'm getting a secretary in a week or so, then we'll get on swimmingly. Now fill in this form.'

I filled in the form. He wrote across it, 'Highly recommended' and said, 'I'll send it to the town right away so you'll be able to start work in three days.'

He shuffled his papers and shouted to nobody in particular, 'Bring me the suspect Serduke.'

My heart missed a beat. I was going to witness an interrogation. Even now, after three years during which my heart has turned to stone, it gives me the shudders to think of that interrogation.

As they brought in the suspect Gus whispered to me, 'Observe and learn.'

He leaned over the desk and buried his nose in the papers. I stopped breathing. Pertsman went on worrying his tablecloth. That minute of tense silence felt like an eternity to me. Suddenly Gus jumped to his feet and thumped the desk with all his might.

I was terrified.

'Where are the planks?' Gus shouted in a rasping voice.

'I don't know,' the suspect whispered and, pressing his hands to his chest, said a little prayer.

'I'm asking you, where are the planks?'

'But I . . .'

'Where are the planks? Tell me. I know everything. Where did you hide them?'

'I swear I don't know. Ask uncle Mitro, comrade. He'll tell you I stayed at home all that day.'

'Where are the planks?'

The suspect prayed. Gus ran in circles around him, making the desk shudder with his fist. I was afraid to move. Pertsman went on glueing. Gus kept asking with the diligence of a faulty gramophone, 'Where are the planks? Tell me! Where are the planks? Tell me! Where are the planks? Tell me!'

The suspect went on praying.

Gus sat down and began to leaf through the file. He was obviously considering a change of tack. Pertsman folded up the tablecloth and began to stuff it into an envelope the size of a child's coffin.

Gus brushed his hair back with a shaking hand and cleared his throat. His eyes filled with tears. He said with feeling, 'Ah, Serduke, Serduke . . . You were such a good peasant . . . No, no, don't get up . . . It's sad, very sad . . . So you insist that you know nothing about the planks you stole . . . that is, borrowed? No?'

'That's right,' the suspect said swallowing. 'I don't know.'

'I see,' Gus said. 'But I do know. And since you refuse to tell me, I'll tell you. On the night of June the thirteenth, persons unknown stole five pine planks from citizen Gogovich of the village of Vasilyevka. It's a petty theft. However, what concerns us is neither the quantity of the stolen goods nor their quality. What concerns us is the principle. Do you follow me?'

'Of course I do,' the suspect said. 'I follow you very well. Only I . . .'

'Well,' Gus went on. 'How did it happen? This is how it happened: a certain peasant called Serduke, a good family man without prior record, without realising what he was doing while being, shall I say, under the influence, said to his crony . . . you know the chap . . . his name escapes me.'

Gus snapped his fingers staring at his prey.

'What's his name?'

'I don't know.'

Gus made a wry face.

'Alright, we'll call him X. So he said to X, "Listen, X, why don't we go to Gogovich and take five of his pine planks?" "Alright," X said. "Let's go to Gogovich and take five of his pine planks." They went. It was the night of June the thirteenth. It was a moonless night. Dogs barked somewhere.' (Gus gave me a wink.) 'Serduke and X climbed over the fence and approached the shed. Gogovich's dog began to bark. Serduke and X broke the lock, entered the shed, took the planks and carried them off the above Gogovich's holding. Immediately afterwards they hid the planks. I know where they hid the planks. I know very well where they hid the planks. But I don't want to say it. I want you to say it. Why do I want you to say it? This is why—because I feel sorry for you. I feel sorry for your wasted youth. I feel sorry for your abandoned wife. I feel sorry for your tiny children who will clutch at . . . at whatever and cry, "Where is our father?" Yes, it's not the planks we're concerned with. After all what are a few planks? Nothing. Especially as I know where they are and can get them back any time. But what will happen to you? They'll lock you up in prison. Not because you've taken the planks but because you refuse to

admit it. If you confess I'll let you go right away. Otherwise I'll have to lock you up in prison. Just say two words—I confess, and you're free. Well?'
'I confess,' the suspect whispered and waved his hand.
'Splendid. I knew you'd confess.'
Gus gave me a look of triumph. The suspect rose looking at the door.
'Can I go now?'
'Wait a minute. Where are the planks?'
'You know where they are, comrade. I don't know because I didn't steal them.'
'But you said I confess.'
'I don't know.'
Gus jumped up and thumped his desk.
'Why the hell have you been pulling my leg all this time?'
The polite suspect was silent.
Gus produced a sheet of paper and dipped his pen into the ink-well.
'Then, Serduke, we'll do it the official way. What's your name?'
'Motorny.'
I looked at Gus in terror. A poisonous smirk played on his face. He hissed, 'What? Are you trying to tell me that you're hiding under the name of Motorny? Is that it?'
The suspect fell to his knees.
'Your excellency . . . Comrade. I swear.' He made the sign of the cross. 'I'm Motorny. Pavlo. Ask in the village, anybody will tell you. Vaska Serduke was in the same cell as me. It's true, I did a bit of bootlegging. I confess. But to steal—no, I don't have the nerve.' He burst into sobs.
Gus walked around the desk whistling 'Two grenadiers to France . . .' He avoided my eyes.
They took Motorny away and Gus shouted to nobody in particular, 'Bring me Serduke! Do you understand? Serduke!'
I tiptoed out of the room.

1927

Viktor Ardov
(1900–1976)

The son of an engineer, Ardov was educated as an economist. His father was shot at the beginning of the Revolution. Soon afterwards Ardov published his first stories in a satirical magazine. From 1925 he wrote mostly for variety shows.

The Bloodthirsty Profession

A shy young man entered the office, politely wiped his feet on the doormat, jerked his shoulders to adjust his jacket, and gave a delicate cough.

The denizen of the office, who sat at a wardrobe-like desk, raised his head and looked at the young man.

'Oh, it's you. Good. I've got some work for you . . . Take a seat . . . I'll show you. I've got it written down somewhere. Here we are. Look, my dear fellow, when are you going to bump off this Professor Mokin?'

'As soon as he finishes his invention. I've got people following him. As soon as he writes it all down we'll . . .'

'But you can't. It's too early, my dear boy. Let us see his machine in action first. Then we'll be perfectly justified in finishing him off. Not before.'

'Well, perhaps you're right. We can wait.'

'Definitely! Another thing, it would be a good idea if Zherebtsov broke a leg. You know, your province is full of pot-holes, ditches—it shouldn't be difficult. Will you organise for him to break a leg?'

'Yes, sir. We can do it.'

'Now it would help if that woman—what's her name?—Prilipaeva—also died. Only quietly, without fuss, without causing suspicion, if you see what I mean.'

'Oh yes, of course!'

'See to it, will you? Now, what are we going to do with Uprelov's money? The only way I can see is to burgle him. Yes, the simplest way to get hold of his money is to burgle him. Can you do that?'

'I don't see why not. We can burgle him. He shares a flat with some old crone. I'll send a couple of boys. Should be easy.'

'That's that then. Now, Katushkevich. You know what? I think the best way to get rid of him is to infect him with some disease. Cholera, for instance, or malignant anthrax.'

'May I object, sir, if you don't mind? Cholera or anthrax won't do. If we had to organise an epidemic, cholera would be perfect, but for one person typhoid fever is best. Especially spotted. The fever, I mean . . .'

'Alright, let it be typhoid fever. It's all the same to me. Just make sure you don't forget. Find a couple of bacilli and all that. So, that's Katushkevich. Now, Karasuke. Shall we poison him? Yes, I think we'll poison him. Put some cyanide in his food, or maybe rotten fish will do the trick.'

'Sure. We'll slip him a rotten sturgeon in the canteen.'

'Lovely. Well, keep me posted, dear boy. I expect a report from you next week. Incidentally, let Utyatin die as well. To hell with him. One more, one less doesn't make much difference, but I'll feel much safer without him. That's all for now. See you.'

There is no reason for the reader to be terrified by the viciousness and cynicism of the above conference. I swear it's not the conspiracy of a criminal gang but only . . . corrections to a filmscript.

1925

Striving after Friendship

It transpired that the empty room had been given to a professor. The inhabitants of the communal flat were flattered by the rank of their new neighbour, although nobody knew him personally.

On the morning the professor moved in, the front door opened unusually wide to let through a rampant mattress, and behind it the professor's wife, anxious, her hat askew, her arms loaded with bundles. Klavdia Nikiforovna, who lived in the last room down the corridor, stood in the entrance hall offering her smile by way of welcome.

'At long last!' Klavdia Nikiforovna said. 'I simply couldn't wait. I thought, at least there'll be one more intellectual in the flat.' Lowering her voice she added, 'Without you I've been literally suffocating here . . . such rough public . . . all workers. Greetings to the professor.'

In half an hour, Klavdia Nikiforovna put her head through the professor's door. The head turned, inspecting everything, and whispered, 'One more thing: don't trust the Katins. Their room is the first off the entrance hall. He drinks and she has a lover and a temper.'

In the evening, when the professor and his wife sat in their already tidied room, something rustled in the key-hole and in five seconds their door opened slightly. Again Klavdia Nikiforovna put her head through the door.

'I see your kettle's been boiling. Come and have tea with me. You're welcome, without ceremony, as neighbours and intellectuals.'

The professor declined politely, pleading fatigue.

In the morning the professor's wife noticed the disappearance of a basket she had left in the corridor. The basket turned up on the back stairs, considerably misshapen.

'I put it there,' Klavdia Nikiforovna said drily. 'You refuse me friendship, turn up your nose at my tea . . . In general you seem to have an inflated idea of yourself as a professor. So you've no right to clutter up the corridor!'

During the next three days Klavdia Nikiforovna tried to do mischief to her new neighbours. She put water in their paraffin, hid their crockery, stole their mail, dirtied their furniture and used many other similar devices to avenge her rejected friendship. On the fourth day, quite unexpectedly, Klavdia Nikiforovna's head once again appeared in the professor's room. 'Why is your kettle taking so long to boil? Maybe there's water in your paraffin? You can come and have tea with me. It isn't proper that we intellectuals should be complete strangers. I feel ashamed before people.'

Once again the invitation was declined. Klavdia Nikiforovna at once resumed hostilities with a view to offering peace in a week.

The third stage of the struggle for friendship took a somewhat less intense course. Klavdia Nikiforovna molested the professor lazily, without fancy, as if from habit.

Once, right in the middle of this agony of hostility, the professor had a party. The sight of the jolly guests, their cheerful voices, the bustle of the hosts aroused envy in the entire block of flats.

There was a sharp knock on the professor's door.

'Citizens! It's pretty selfish of you,' they heard Klavdia Nikiforovna's voice. 'It's pretty boorish of you to leave your galoshes in the corridor to make puddles for us!'

After five minutes the knock and the shout were repeated. The guests lapsed into an awkward silence.

The professor's wife went to the kitchen. Trying to contain herself she said to Klavdia Nikiforovna, 'What do you want from us?'

Klavdia Nikiforovna picked up the professor's boiling kettle and emptied it into the sink.

Trembling, the professor's wife repeated, 'What do you want from us?'

'I want to be friends with you. Invite me to your party,' Klavdia Nikiforovna said calmly, and stretched her hand towards the tray carrying the professor's plates.

'Never!'

Without haste Klavdia Nikiforovna chose a cup and threw it to the floor.

'My God . . . What is this? Never!'

Klavdia Nikiforovna lifted a pile of saucers from the tray.

The professor's wife pressed her fingers to her temples. She could hear the renewed conversation in her room. A row would be too loud and it would embarrass her before her guests.

'Alright,' the professor's wife said. 'I give in. Will you come to my party?'

Klavdia Nikiforovna gave her a contemptuous look and, slowly and neatly, put the saucers back on the tray.

'In a minute,' she said cheerfully. 'I'll just change into something more dressy. After all, you've got a lot of intellectual strangers in there.'

In twenty minutes she knocked, this time quietly and delicately, and entered the professor's room, freshly powdered and wearing a lace collar.

'May I introduce,' the professor's wife said, closing her eyes and firmly pressing her hands together, 'our neighbour.'

Klavdia Nikiforovna smiled, demonstrating her gold tooth.

'Oh, so many people! I won't shake hands individually. I'll just say a general how-do-you-do.'

1929

The Hypnotist

The town was small and dirty. The rooms in the hotel were of a similar description. The literature on the harmfulness of rats, which Lukashuk had come to sell there, found no buyers.

Lukashuk even began to entertain doubts as to whether he'd be able to sell enough to pay for his room and leave the town. His last hope of a happy ending collapsed in the office of the local cooperative on which, as the place most abounding with rats, Lukashuk had relied most of all. In reply to Lukashuk's exhortations to buy a brochure entitled 'Not a single rat under a Soviet roof', the manager tactlessly dragged a huge ginger cat from under his desk and, putting it on top of Lukashuk's literature, said, 'This is our brochure. We need no other.'

Lukashuk pinched his competitor's tail viciously and left.

Gloomily he made his way to the hotel, trying in vain to think of a way out of the situation.

In front of him walked four executives, burdened with their briefcases and discussing topics of local concern.

'Demekhin hasn't come to work?' one executive said.

'He hasn't,' another replied. 'He's been drinking again. And Balakhonov hasn't. And Usachev from the seventh stall. They always go on the binge together.'

'These binges are a regular pest!' the first executive said. 'People say that in Moscow they are treating alcoholism with hypnosis. If only we had a hypnotist here.'

A third executive agreed, 'That's true. I'd be the first to take the cure.'

'Me too,' the second executive said.

'And me!'

'What do you want it for? You don't drink.'

'I don't drink but my brother-in-law does. I'd pass on to him whatever treatment they gave me. If only we had a hypnotist.'

Lukashuk swallowed twice, clutched his head and ran to his hotel. The attendant, bribed with Lukashuk's last half-rouble, nailed a notice to the front door announcing that a visiting hypnotist in room four offered a guaranteed cure from alcoholism for the moderate fee of one rouble. The success of the notice was most heartening. In twenty minutes a respectful hand knocked on the door.

Lukashuk, who had completed his preparations, (a clean towel borrowed from the attendant, twenty copies of 'Not a single rat under a Soviet roof' in the way of scientific literature, a can opener playing the role of a menacing medical instrument, and an account book transformed into a register of patients), bade the visitor enter.

A brown shoe of monumental dimensions moved into the room and above it, at a height of seven feet, a fur hat with ear flaps. Directly under the hat there was a mighty moustache in which two matches and an apple core had perished.

Lukashuk opened the register and enquired earnestly, 'Name? How long have you been drinking?'

'Prunin. Since I was seven.'

Lukashuk doodled with a pencil, wagged his head and approached the moustache, which had sat down in a corner. He waved his hand in front of the moustache, gave a piercing whistle, clicked his tongue and, in conclusion, did three steps of a tap dance with his left foot.

'Don't you dare drink any more! Do you hear me?'

The moustache, trying to burrow into the wall, whispered timidly, 'Forgive me, I won't . . .'

'I bet you won't,' Lukashuk said, stepping back and sighing. 'Give me a rouble. Congratulations, you've been cured.'

The moustache, twitching joyously and dropping the matches and the apple core, counted coppers.

Encouraged by success, Lukashuk, like a proper physician, washed his hands, opened the door and called, 'Next please! Money first.'

A smallish queue had formed in the corridor. There was even a person with a baby attempting to jump the queue.

Lukashuk plunged into his practice. He entered the patients in the account book, took their roubles and only then hypnotised them for all he was worth.

'Drinking?' he screamed at his patients. 'Guzzling? Sucking vodka? I'll show you, you son of a bitch!'

In front of his patients' noses Lukashuk hissed, whistled, boomed, kicked his feet, hopped, gyrated on one foot. He kicked one of them, tickled another's belly, pulled the hair of a third. He gave two ringing slaps in the face to a patient who seemed a bit more thick-skinned than the others.

'If you get sozzled once more I'll terrorise you to death!'

The pile of copper, silver and notes in the warped drawer of the desk grew nicely. The patients crawled out of the room, terrified and shattered by the hypnotist's magnetic power. In a word, it was a most satisfactory procedure.

However, Lukashuk began to tire. The meagre nutrition of the past two days and the purely physical methods of his treatment began to take their toll. Therefore when the eighteenth patient entered the room Lukashuk suddenly lost his energy. All he could manage was a shake of the head.

'Tut-tut. It's not nice, is it? You ought to give up drink, you know.'

The eighteenth patient swayed and, producing a bottle from his inner pocket, asked, 'Will you share the last one with me?'

'Alright, if it's the last one,' the exhausted Lukashuk said, thinking that a glass of vodka might strengthen him for further work.

The patient fussily washed the glass which stood by, half-filled it and handed it to Lukashuk.

'To your hypnotism!'

'Thank you. And to your cure from drink!'

Lukashuk's head filled with a slight humming and he was reluctant to part from such a nice eighteenth patient for the sake of those who waited in the corridor. Wishing to postpone that unpleasant moment, Lukashuk suggested, 'Shall we have another go?'

They had another go. In fact they had two other goes. Then it turned out that there was nothing left for a third go.

'Take back your rouble which you gave me for your cure,' Lukashuk said after some thought. 'Go and get some more vodka. While you're at it get some sausage and pickle. One doesn't run into such a nice fellow very often.'

The queue became agitated when the eighteenth patient had dived through it twice on his way for more vodka. By that time Lukashuk was beyond caring.

'Be quiet, will you!' he barked. 'Can't you see I'm busy hypnotising. It's an especially difficult case. The citizen doesn't want to give up drinking.'

The queue could see for themselves the truth of the last statement when the eighteenth patient went to the wine shop yet again. The hypnotist put out his head and shouted, 'Don't stint yourself! Get two bottles. And forget the pickles!'

Then the queue listened attentively to the hypnotist singing 'Ala-verdy' and attempting to organise his feet into a folk dance.

After the folk dance the hypnotist put out his head again and announced with a decisive hiccup, 'What are you standing there for? Can't you see the surgery has been postponed till tomorrow?'

The queue quickly skedaddled while the hypnotist, ever quicker, got fuddled. At least that was how the hotel attendant described his behaviour when a policeman appeared on hearing the window panes being smashed by the hypnotist and the nice eighteenth patient. At this juncture the hypnotist, utterly drunk, was screaming, 'Aha! I'll show you how to drink! I'll show you how to breed rats! Aha! Not a single rat under a Soviet roof!'

Lukashuk woke up in a police cell. His hypnotising activities had completely evaporated from his memory. On the contrary, the cell's atmosphere had strengthened his zeal for his former profession.

To the police officer who questioned him he said, 'Comrade, I'll tell you from my personal experience: your cell is so teeming with rats that you must undoubtedly buy a brochure "Not a single rat under a Soviet roof" Undoubtedly!'

The officer declined the suggestion as irrelevant to the case.

1930

Andrey Platonov (1899–1951)

Platonov came from a working class family and served in the Red Army during the Civil War. After the war he graduated from a polytechnic institute and worked as a land reclamation and electrical engineer. He published his first stories in 1918 and became a professional writer in 1927.

In the mid-1930s Stalin's personal dislike of Platonov's writing resulted in his works being declared anti-Soviet and his name was removed from the official history of Soviet literature. Living in poverty, Platonov caught tuberculosis from his son who had, in turn, caught it in a labour camp, and he died in 1951.

The Whirlpool

I. Early life and growing up

Somewhere, sometime, there lived a man called Evdok or Evdokim. His family name was Ababurenko, but friends called him simply Baklazhanov.

At school a priest taught him to make the sign of the cross (forehead, chest, right shoulder, left shoulder) but failed. Evdok repeated after him in his own fashion: forehead, liver . . .

'What do we call St. Mary?'

'The Verdant . . .'

'The Virgin Mary, you scarecrow! You've got neither brain nor faith. You'll grow up an infidel, an Abdul-Hamid.'

'Count from the beginning,' the schoolmistress said to Evdokim. 'Count on your fingers.'

Evdokim counted thoughtfully, without haste, 'One, two, three, one more, thumb . . .'

'Sit down, you fool,' the schoolmistress said. 'Listen to the others count.'

Evdok couldn't wait to get back home. He missed his mother and feared that their house might catch fire in his absence, what with the weather being hot, dry and windy, and that she might get trapped inside. The whistle blew—twelve o'clock. Father must have come home to dinner. The grass and burdocks in Stepanikha's kitchen garden had grown awfully tall. The boys must be catching birds. It would be evening soon and the mosquitoes would come.

There was a bucket at school, to drink from. Every day they were taught the Scriptures, then the schoolmistress Apollinaria Nikolaevna came and drew straight lines on the blackboard. Evdok scrawled in his book what looked like birch twigs. She made him read aloud.

Evdok peered at the textbook and read, 'Mo, mmo . . .'

During the breaks the watchman Dmitrich came so that the kids wouldn't smash a window or commit other excesses.

If someone cried because of a fight or from missing their mother,

Dmitrich bawled, 'Back! Get to work!'

Many days passed. The school dog Volchok died. Evdokim's father bought another samovar in the flea market. Evdokim's little brother Sanya was born. All summer Evdok pushed him about in a little cart. By St. Peter's day he had died of stomach trouble.

Evdokim's heart began to beat faster. On summer evenings he went into the fields and yearned for the distant woods, a star, far-away empty country roads.

When Evdok grew up he became a soldier. He marched on the parade ground waving his rifle and a heavy immovable weight lay in his heart. Once a strange thing happened to him: he didn't have a shit for seven days. When he went to bed his stomach rumbled as water sloshed about in it senselessly. He was surrounded by bunks, snoring, swearing, stinking while inside him there were country roads in evening cool and his mother waiting for him with dinner.

He could've socked on the jaw the one who invented the human heart!

Screwing up his courage he went to see the doctor. 'This thing happened to me.'

'Wha-at?' the doctor wailed.

Evdok tried again.

'I haven't had a shit for seven days.'

As he was leaving he absentmindedly picked up a pencil from the doctor's desk.

'Take it as a momento, Ababurenko,' the doctor said.

Evdok stroked the doctor's black hat.

'Please, Ababurenko, take it too. You can also have my pen. Do you like it?'

It turned out that the doctor was a hypochondriac. He never touched a door handle unless he was wearing a glove. If you touched anything in his office he gave it to you as a momento: a lamp, a sheet of paper, a cloth or some instrument.

He was strange, but a serious-minded man.

After two days Evdok's bowels unblocked themselves, and he felt better.

Thus Evdokim's life went on, a river of uniform days, until he began to discover the relationship between a star and such things as straw, a fence and an empty nocturnal road between silent villages.

That is a long story and one day it will be made known to the people.

II. The journey

The Revolution came. There was a movement of people on the earth. It was a jolly business. Everybody knows that. Ababurenko was a Commissar. He fed his troops off starving villages. He did a lot of thinking, fighting and travelling. To him the Revolution was a grand journey, a realisation of his hidden soul in the world. He requisitioned poultry and inanimate produce and wrote ultimatums;

> In the name of the Soviet Republic I demand that my troops be paid four months in advance.
>
> Commander-commissar, member of the Bolshevik Party Evdokim Ababurenko.
>
> I warn you that I'll seize your town and bring all the inhabitants, philistines and others, to revolutionary trial according to my revolutionary conscience.
>
> Commissar Ababurenko N7143268.

Ababurenko's name resounded among the peasants of the steppe and was forgotten. Everything passed, as if drowned in a whirlpool in some Tatar river.

Evdokim was homeless, so he took up tailoring. He settled in a small town and made a bosom friend, Elpidifor Mamashin, who was a bass and a fool.

Elpidifor* and I went to Evdokim's hovel—we had business with him, nothing very important. It was silent, dark and scary.

'Where is the tailor? I want my trousers made into riding breeches.'

'Hang on,' Elpidifor cried. 'I know: a living man smells.'

We sniffed around. First the air was clear, then, indeed, we smelled tobacco and singed beard.

'Here he is. Get out of there!'

The bed creaked and an invisible lean body blew its nose and gurgled. To make some light, and out of politeness, I lit a quiet cigarette.

'Hullo, Evdokim! Wake up!'

'Greetings, citizens.' It sounded like the blow of a sledge-hammer. That voice had been preserved in the clear air, silence and darkness. Like a cucumber in a barrel in winter.

We lit a sooty lamp. There was a bench, a table, a bucket of water and a goldfinch soundly asleep in the warmth under the ceiling. To add seriousness and the weight of his profession to the occasion, Evdokim put on his glasses, tying them to his ears with a string, a home-made device.

*Elpidifor was a relative of mine.

He had grown older, more morose and quiet. He made one think of an old man, of sleep and bread—brown, tender and warm like the inside of a loaf. He seemed to be made of leather; if you scratched his cheek a scar would remain. But in his yellow eyes there flickered mischief and disquiet. He was a randy devil, a trouble-maker and a singer who strutted about like a cock. On Sundays he treated unmarried girls to lemonade. According to him he hadn't married because he had failed to find a suitably tender woman, so he had bought the goldfinch.

'So you want riding breeches?'

'Yes, that's what I'd like.'

'I see . . . This is enough for one leg. If you want two you'll have to buy more cloth,' Evdokim said thoughtfully, looking through his glasses.

'How much would you say it's going to cost?'

'I'd say one million.'*

'Splendid, splendid,' Elpidifor said, (he was a kind of former intellectual). 'See you later.'

'Goodbye. Do you want a light?'

'Don't trouble yourself. We'll find the way out.'

We climbed the hill towards the ancient monastery. It was amazing how the houses stood there—on stilts and on rocks. Sewage flowed down here from the town. If someone urinated above, spray flew into Evdokim's window. Life was unhealthy in that dangerous location. In the spring and during the rainy season Evdokim and his neighbours were stranded on an island and newspapers reported their plight, although they never read newspapers. In the old days the police used to evict the population every spring. But they wouldn't go, climbing on their roofs instead and dragging with them their children, pigs, a cock, a samovar. When the water rose at night and chairs floated off irretrievably and a calf was drowned, the people on the roofs would raise a wail.

In the morning a policeman would shake his fist from the hill.

'I told you. I warned you, You just can't let go of your rubbish. Now you'll fast, you flunkeys of the devil!'

After a day or two, when the water subsided, the policeman would come down and give someone a beating.

Those were the days!

The next day Elpidifor bought his own trousers in the flea market, recognising a stamp on them. He went to see Evdokim with the intention of beating him up but Evdokim had gone. That was the end of it.

On his way to his village Evdokim chuckled, 'You have funny ways, God!'

*In that distant time simple people dealt in billions and thousands of thousands.

He came to his village, sold his grandmother's house and bought a horse. He took the horse to the Don to wash and it drowned.

'It's a shame about the animal,' Evdok said, and went on some other business.

He stayed in the village for a week or two until he ran out of food. Then he went begging. He walked all over the place in his sadness.

Autumn came. The wind howled in the telegraph wires. With a sack of potatoes on his back Evdokim walked past the ancient wind-swept hills. He was old and there was nobody to love and pity him. It seemed to him that all the sorrow in the world was only kept in check by some light weight and one day all the people would suddenly burst into tears and cling together. It would happen when a flood, a drought or some plague came, or when a host of rebelling animals came out of the Siberian woods. Man gets nothing but sorrow from his heart.

Evdok became a tramp and a beggar. He understood and loved many things with a melancholy love.

In a remote village, in a hollow, an old woman gave Evdok shelter.

'Stay here, old man. I've got some potatoes. You can't go out now in these clothes. Put your stick in the corner.'

Evdok stayed with the old woman until spring. All winter both of them groaned every night from the cold, hunger and old festering sorrows. Evdok's heart filled with longing. He looked out of the window—the snow, the river, the graveyard on a hill, a quiet day coming to an end.

Where could one go when there was infinity around!

In the spring, water roared in the hollow. Then the roads dried out and sparrows appeared in the village street. Evdok got ready to go.

'Is there anything you need?' the old woman asked.

'No,' Evdok said.

'Good luck then.'

'Goodbye, Lukerya.'

Evdok set off.

The wind was gentle and quiet like tender, heart-felt music. On top of a bald hill, washed by water and air, Evdok took a deep breath, looking at the distant forest border, at everything that was alive, melancholy and faraway. Then he climbed down and drank water from a free-running stream.

His days began all over again.

III. Death

Evdokim Ababurenko took the patronymic of Solomon. He wanted to be called Solomonovich not because he was of Jewish origin but because he was a beggar and an orphan of ancestry unknown. Also the last summer before the Revolution he had worked for a rag-and-bone man, Solomon Luperden, a Jew.

However, it was all in the past.

Solomon was no more, he must have died. His nineteen children had been scattered in obscurity all over the world.

Khannochka, Solomon's wife, a kind and beautiful woman, had died of starvation two years ago when the cossacks had taken their town. Some people said two wicked officers had driven a stick into her womb and that was why she died.

It was all in the past now.

Let us save the living. As for the dead, we'll mourn them in solitude at night. A red sign hung now over Solomon's warehouse:

> R.S.F.S.R.
> Central Warehouse
> of the
> Bone-working
> Cotton-wool
> and Paper
> Industry
> of Regional Status
> *   *   *
> Painted by the artist Pupkov.

Solomon had operated without any sign—he was known well enough without it. His life had been tolerable—the bustle and hard work of the office and the cool and sweetness of the eight little rooms of his house, which smelled of his wife's fecundity.

All that had happened long ago, before the Revolution. Now Abubarenko was an old man himself. Apart from being an old man he was an orator, a musician, a lover of animals and a philosopher contemplating the good of humankind. In other words, as he used to say, he was a kind of Bolshevik, a member of the all-Russian Communist Party (of Bolsheviks), the last words in brackets. That was how he explained who he was to those who didn't know.

Ababurenko was an imposing person, a man of substance.

His life had flown past like a gust of wind. There had been frosts and storms, warmth and affection, an occasional moment of contentment. Very nice indeed! Like high, almost invisible clouds, there floated in his memory dear faces, Khanna's generous hands, the loving eyes of Daryushka, his common-law wife who had refused to marry him because of his loose tongue.

However, when Evdokim Solomonovich looked at his life he saw nothing but propriety. It is in a living man's power to eliminate impropriety from his life.

He had personally set fire to Prince Baratynsky's house. He regretted having let the old man escape. He would like to have spilled the prince's guts. The old bastard had been such a pest to the peasants. He had been like a roach in your pants, a small bother that never stopped tickling. Another thing he would dearly like to have done was to have given hell to the foreigners. That would have been great fun! Evdokim Solomonovich knew a thing or two about the foreigners. He hadn't gone to school for nothing.

For some reason in his old age Evdokim Solomonovich became a great lover of sugar. He was now a watchman in a kitchen garden, an extremely boring occupation. It's all very well for a tree or some other plant to spend its entire life in one place without getting bored. A man is a moving thing, he can even swim, and so sitting in one place is boring to him, even frightening.

But it couldn't be helped, and Evdokim Solomonovich spent his days boiling potatoes. He ate them with a lot of sugar. Then, since the fire was still burning, he would cook a stew and eat it with a lot of sugar too, although without much appetite. Then he would hang the pot over the fire again and lie for a while on his stomach. Thus, in unceasing eating and contemplation, he spent the summer days and starry nights with a dead moon.

Evdokim Solomonovich suffered from hydrophobia and also heartburn; therefore he did not bathe, although the river was within a mile. Because of his dirtiness, lice multiplied on him, but he got used to it and it didn't bother him much.

Autumn was approaching. The mosquitoes were gone. Instead there appeared wolves, old and young ones. Evdokim Solomonovich was fond of howling like a wolf. Some people played the mandolin, others played a pipe, but he was an artist at howling. He did it so well that the wolves came and climbed on top of his dug-out. Holy terror!

When the wolves left the boredom returned and Evdokim Solomonovich howled again. The fear and the howling, human and lupine, made the nights seem shorter.

However, the nights grew longer and colder. In the mornings the air was transparent and resonant. The chimneys kept smoking long into the day—there was no reason to hurry with breakfast. The fields lay dead. There was nowhere to hurry, all work was finished. The only thing to do was to dig up potatoes.

One night—no big deal—Evdokim Solomonovich died.

He had gone to bed early. At night he got up to have a pee and crawled out of his dug-out. The moon stood over the white empty field which was covered in icy dew. The deserted soulless world where man forgot other men's existence. Far away a night-watchman rattled his rattle and the tree-tops made a grumbling noise.

For some reason Evdokim Solomonovich sat down on the ground. He felt his head roll back and strength drain out of his body. But his heart didn't upset him any more.

Evdokim Solomonovich jumped to his feet. He wanted to cry and to say something, but he fell and hit the ground so hard that his stomach rumbled.

To his surprise the moon went dark before his eyes. The stars darted past in a noisy stream and the ground caved in under him like the bottom of a dried-up Tatar river.

The watchman stopped rattling in the village as if he had never been there at all, or perhaps had fallen asleep on his feet.

1927

Yury Olesha
(1899–1960)

Olesha was the only son of a middle-class Polish Catholic family. He studied law at Novorossiisk University and in 1919 he volunteered for the Red Army. After the Civil War he worked as a journalist on the railwaymen's magazine 'Whistle'. He published his first story in 1924 and in 1927 wrote his finest novel, *Envy*. This was followed by plays, short stories and another novel, *Three Fat Men*. With the onset of Socialist Realism in the 1930s Olesha fell silent.

The Legend

At night soldiers entered the building to carry out a massacre. I was woken up by shots. They were shooting somewhere upstairs, on the fourth floor.

While the soldiers were busy two floors up, while they were coming down the stairs to burst in on us, the following happened to me—

Firstly: I found myself in my parents' bedroom (for the first time at night). I saw my parents' bedroom at night. A lamp under a pink shade burned on the bed-side table. I saw my parents together in one bed. My father appeared to me to be in a shameless state. Moreover, he acted in such a way as to reveal my mother in a similar state. In order to get off the bed my father, who occupied the side against the wall, had to climb over my mother. He began to climb, pulling the blanket after him. My mother was left without a cover. She just lay there making no effort to hide herself. Her mind was befuddled with fear.

(I felt no pity. I should have lifted the blanket, covered her, put my arms round her, stroked her head. With some words or other I should somehow have inspired confidence in my father, restored his self-possession. I did nothing of the kind.)

Secondly: I thought of my father in the following way—

It has never occurred to you that you may be less intelligent than I. You will never admit even the possibility of discussing equality or inequality between children and parents. You think you are my ideal. You think that I want to be like you. You think that I want to be a continuation of you, your features, your moustache, your gestures, your thoughts, your bedroom, that I should also want to lie with a woman as you lie with my mother. You think that's the way it should be. I don't want to be a continuation of you! Do you hear?

Thirdly: Suddenly I saw in a different way all the furniture that had surrounded me for so many years, and the sight shattered me. Every article forced its kinship on me. A round clock hung on the wall. 'I was born to its chimes,' my mother had said many times. 'So was your grandmother.' The clock was a tradition, it was a legend. I don't want any legends. I don't want to die to the chimes of this clock. I don't want to be a continuation. Suddenly I realised with clarity—I was surrounded by a family council of furniture. The furniture counselled me, taught me how to live. The sideboard was saying to me, 'I shall follow you in life. I shall stand behind you. I'll last a long time, I'm durable. Two generations have kept food in me. Treat me with care and I'll serve you, your son and your grandson. I'll become a legend.'

Suddenly I understood my dependance on these objects. The round table forced me to turn when I wanted to walk straight. The wardrobe moved me to the left when I wanted to move to the right. The lacquered shelves on the wall restricted the waving of my arms. Many times I had wanted to revolt. But my father mediated between me and the furniture. He had secret instructions from the sideboards and the gramophones on how to cheat and appease me, how to prevent me from entertaining thoughts of war, how to make me behave. Sometimes some curtain, in fear for the entire realm, would give me a bribe in the form of a velvet ball which had been torn off a cord. I would throw the ball any way I wanted, violating the traditions and the legends. I could assign it any function, however inconsistent with the family's idea of what a curtain was, how it should be treated and what place it was to occupy in human life . . .

Fourthly: I betrayed my father.

My father came running out of the bedroom. He was shaking. He couldn't speak. From fear he had ceased to be a human being. He had turned into a chicken. He was flying! He flew onto the table (in his underwear), stayed there for a moment, took off again, landed on the sideboard, then on the window sill, like a chicken chased by a cook.

After all this (not flying—he wasn't flying—I just felt dizzy and in my dizziness that was how I perceived the external manifestation of his fear) he attempted to gain control over himself.

His attempt was successful. He changed at once, stopped flying, planted his feet on the ground, raised his head, put his hand on my shoulder and said, 'Kolya, you must be proud. We'll die like noblemen.'

In other words my father's power continued, the council of furniture had not been dispersed, the legend still existed. The paterfamilias, the propagator of our kind, the guardian of tradition, showed his last trick. He would die historically. He would make himself a martyr.

'Wait,' my father went on. 'I'll be right with you. We'll die together.'

He went into the bedroom and returned dragging my mother. He tried to lift her to her feet but she collapsed. They were both covered by my father's regulation overcoat.

'Button up,' he ordered me (I had my student jacket thrown over my shoulders). 'We'll meet death with dignity.'

They banged on the door. My father went to open it. My mother lay on the floor. He walked like a martyr. He carried his back, his raised shoulders like a tablet. He was already a legend.

I beat him to it. I opened the door and shouted, 'Shoot! Shoot! At the bedroom! At the secret! At the sideboard, at the legend, at all the buttons! Sever me from him, from his moustache, from his thoughts. Liberate me.'

Shouting this I fell submissively into someone's arms. I quietened down as I realised that getting out of bed and becoming so agitated while being sick with typhus might end in catastrophe.

1927

The Prophet

Kozlenkov stood on a hill. It was a hot summer day—immensity, purity, brilliance. In the immensity stood Kozlenkov completely alone, without care, in a cotton blouse, sandals, a cap worn in the summer fashion. His face was growing noticeably sun-tanned. There was a scarcity of foliage. The landscape was somewhat dry. Black fissures showed in the ground. The ground was resonant.

Up the steep path leading to Kozlenkov's pedestal, an angel was climbing briskly, a huge angel, mighty, without wings, with curly black hair reaching to his shoulders. He wore a dressing gown of a dark red material and held a staff in his hand; his knees moved sharply under the dressing gown.

He rose before Kozlenkov on the edge of the hill. His tall staff with blossoming bright-green buds prodded the dry ground between the blades of grass. The staff shone the way furniture shines. The buds looked like nestlings' heads . . . The angel stood straight. His Adam's apple was shaped like a goblet. The angel stretched his hand towards Kozlenkov's shoulder.

At that point Kozlenkov woke up. He woke up, as he always woke up, about eight o'clock in the morning. The remnants of the last night's supper showed green on the table: spring onions, lettuce. Kozlenkov gulped down a glass of water.

He washed and dressed; it was a cheerful summer morning. Kozlenkov looked out of the window. He thought he saw dew glittering somewhere in the greenery, a fluttering bird taking a drop. Any sign of water gladdened him; after the spring onions, thirst had tormented him all night. A neighbour woman ran up and down the corridor, hiding and yelping.

Having drunk tea he came out of the house. The janitor said a girl had hanged herself next door. Kozlenkov hastened to have a look.

The house next door had a little garden in the middle of its front yard. Tenants looked out of the windows. Kozlenkov thought, I'll be late for work. However, he gave in. The incident had taken place in the backyard. Kozlenkov stopped in the arch. A procession moved towards him: women,

men in waistcoats, with baskets of vegetables and brooms, dogs, children. On their hands they carried the girl they had taken out of the noose.

She lay on top of the procession, alive, brightly lit by the sun, in a dress printed with roses. A siren hooted in the distance. An ambulance was coming. Kozlenkov made enquiries: the girl had been unhappy, abandoned, starved.

For some reason Kozlenkov saw a dark window, unopened after the winter, wadding between its worsted frames, a candle. The window had nothing to do with the suicide. Then: an old woman in her dotage sat on a porch. The old woman was eating, picking up bits of food from her lap.

'Sorrow,' Kozlenkov thought. 'Ah, sorrow.'

He felt pity for everybody.

'I must help!' he said loudly, with fervour.

He wanted to say the following, 'I have seen human sorrow. I must help all people at once. I must do something at once which would obliterate human sorrow altogether.'

'They'll help her. She's alive,' they answered him from the crowd.

Kozlenkov did not possess that which would destroy human sorrow at once. He knew there was no such force. One had to wait, to accumulate this force. Kozlenkov's desire was so passionate, his impulse so uncontrollable, that he could not agree to so much as a single minute's wait. Therefore he thought of a miracle.

'I must bring about a miracle,' he sighed.

In the office, during the lunch break, chewing a sausage sandwich, Kozlenkov remembered the morning's incident. Tears glittered in his eyes. He restrained himself from weeping; swallowing became difficult. He imagined a picture.

He enters the yard with a blossoming staff. Birds sing in the garden, flowers sway in the bushes, people run in fear from their window sills. They carry the girl towards him. The old woman can be seen in the arch, also the window with the worsted frame. He touches the girl's forehead with his hand. At once the window rises, turns towards air and sun, opens wide, geraniums hanging from its sill, the wind blowing its curtains. At once the old woman regains both her youth and her son. They eat a water melon sitting at a clean-scrubbed wooden table. The water melon is snowy, scarlet, its seeds clean, shining. You could play tiddly-winks with the seeds. And the girl . . . Everybody is happy. Dreams come true, losses are made good.

Kozlenkov rose. He remembered his dream. His chair stepped back with a rumble. The pages of an account book reared.

He opened the door and stepped over the doorstep into the next room. All the heads were bowed down. He could see open windows and, beyond the windows, greenery, branches. At once all the windows were set in motion—some force, some spirit flew at them, flinging them in all directions. The branches rose and rustled. Papers flew from the desks, forming a whirl-wind. The door behind him slammed shut. The door opposite opened of its own accord.

And, the most important thing, he saw all the heads bowing down, prostrating themselves. Of course he knew the draught was the reason for that. But he also saw that nobody was able to raise their eyes to him. He was free to attach to that any meaning he liked.

He thought, 'They're all prostrating themselves before me. I'm coming. I've seen an angel. I'm a prophet. I'm to perform a miracle.' He walked through a row of rooms producing draughts, a storm. He was followed by screams. The screams meant:

'Watch out! The door! The door! Catch the papers! That window is going to smash! We have no porters here!'

But nobody had forbidden Kozlenkov to hear a different meaning in the screams. Some of them seemed to him an expression of triumph, others—of wrath. He was coming as a prophet, long-awaited by some, hateful to others. He carried out the will of the one who had sent him.

The windows banged, the panes flashed, sending lightning darting into the garden. He had reached the state of ecstasy. He stood before the head of the organisation. He was slowly rising from his armchair towards Kozlenkov. The prophet stood with his hair ruffled by the draught, his eyes burning, pale and panting.

'I want my wages two weeks in advance,' Kozlenkov said. He returned in a minute holding an order from the head of the organisation.

'Miracle!' people were saying around him. 'Miracle! He got his wages by a miracle!'

He received the money. He left the building. Everybody ran to the windows. He walked without his hat, attracting attention.

Then he looked for the girl who had been taken out of the noose. In the backyard he was told that the girl was in hospital. A stranger punched him.

'You're beating the wrong man,' a woman said. 'What are you beating this one for?'

The stranger punched him again between his shoulder blades. The punch straightened Kozlenkov's back. With his back straightened Kozlenkov trotted down the stairs. His face was radiant. He knew he had been taken for another man, the one who had caused the girl's suffering. He didn't protest because he had taken on himself the other's guilt. Ridiculed, he ran across the yard.

In the garden a girl played with a ball. The ball fell into the bushes. Kozlenkov crawled across the grass, the black soil of the flower bed, parted the bushes and picked up the ball. The janitor saw all this from the roof. Kozlenkov's head was wreathed in petals, a thorn stuck in his hand. The janitor, high up and brightly lit, thundered at the world. His curses flew from the heights. His apron flapped, curling into a scroll similar to those held by marble angels. The janitor stood by the top of the fire escape, an ordinary fire escape which seemed to be on fire in the sun. And Kozlenkov felt terror.

Kozlenkov was approaching the hospital. The petals, circling quietly, fell from his head.

'I can't do it,' he sighed. 'Why did they send me an angel?'

He went home. The laundress Fedora sat by the porch in the yard. She was selling vegetables. On the porch stood a basket with heads of cabbage which were rough but looked as if they had been sculpted. Kozlenkov took a closer look. A cabbage head with its leaves curled. These curls, with their marble hardness and the coolness of the leaves, produced agitation in Kozlenkov's memory. He had seen curls of such sculptural quality in the janitor's apron.

The laundress held a cabbage ball. She was dressed in red, she was mighty. The day before, she had stood over her basket in the same way, at the same hour, and Kozlenkov had bought spring onions from her. Now he did the same. The laundress put the cabbage head in the basket (the head squeaked in her hands as if freshly washed) and took out onions. 'A bad laundress,' Kozlenkov thought. Last night when he had gone to bed he had been upset by the harshness of the sheets. He had also eaten a lot of spring onions. At night he had been woken up by thirst. Tormented by the heat, he had turned the pillow over and when, suffering and sleepy, he had gained its other, cool side, comfort and peace came. But soon that side too had become suffused with heat.

The amazing day had come to an end. In the evening, yet again, Kozlenkov ate spring onions. Buttered bread and spring onions—bitter-sweet, sweaty, with an arm-pit smell. Before he got into the bed he groped over the sheet stretched over the mattress in order to smooth out its invisible roughness.

The day had been terrible. Kozlenkov fell asleep. Once again he was tormented by thirst, dryness. Once again the dryness spread before him, a resonant yellow landscape of porous earth. His body revolted. He tossed, seeking the other side of the pillow; he protested in his sleep; he railed at himself, at his actions while asleep; he protested against himself for climbing that hill yet again . . . He bellowed in his sleep, pummelled the blanket . . .

But once again he stood on that hill and the angel in red, black-haired and mighty, climbed towards him. The moment the vision began a heartburn arose in Kozlenkov's sleeping body. Its progress towards his throat, emerging from the depth of his bowels, coincided with the angel's appearance and ascent in his dream. The knowledge Kozlenkov had acquired during the day, the knowledge of similarities between a large number of things, affected his sleeping mind. Since that knowledge tended to unmask his dream, the dream faded, was ready to die away.

Another moment and the sleeper would wake up . . . Kozlenkov did wake up in a moment, having managed to notice the laundress Fedora on the edge of the hill.

Kozlenkov woke up. It was light. He drank water, laughed and went back to sleep.

1929

Leonid Leonov
(1899–?)

Leonov's father was a self-educated poet and radical journalist of peasant stock and until 1918 Leonov worked on his father's newspaper in Archangel. In 1920 he joined the Red Army and his first story was published two years later. After 1928 Leonov moved from sympathetic neutrality to active support of the Soviet regime, writing a considerable number of novels and plays in the style of Socialist Realism.

The Tramp

The tea was like brewed straw and the sugar tasted of kerosene. Plumping the unfinished cup down on the table Chadaev listened abstractedly to the din of the inn. Towards midday, as was usual on market days, the crush increased, but Chadaev was enveloped in empty silence. Suddenly he rose heavily and, hands outstretched, moved towards the back door. The inn-keeper, who valued the impeccable reputation of his business more than his one eye, followed Chadaev, but his suspicions proved unfounded.

In the smelly, greenish twilight of the backyard, pierced by sun rays, the guest was harnessing his horse. Lazy and relaxed, it parted reluctantly from its tasty oats. The guest didn't mind—he didn't notice. He picked up a chunk of bread dropped by someone on the dirty straw and stared at it for a long time before he put it in his bag. Disappointed in Chadaev's secret, the inn-keeper stepped out of his hiding place and Chadaev felt embarrassed.

'At home only the dogs will meet me,' he said, referring to the bread.

'Who's asking who'll meet you at home?' the inn-keeper replied and went back into the inn, his teasing eye winking.

Chadaev drove out of the yard.

The April afternoon was entangled in the fervent trilling of larks. The puddles rippled blindingly, an elusive babbling filled the air. It endowed the heart with a pleasant, almost tipsy lightness, but to Chadaev his forty-fifth spring seemed an outrage perpetrated by the crazy elements. Pulling out his wife's letter, on account of which he was leaving the provincial capital before time and against reason, he once again tried to comprehend its prickly scrawl. 'My dear husband,' he read mostly from memory, 'I'm bored. My dear husband, I cry every day. My dear husband, I don't know what to do with myself. My dear husband, I've been going out . . .' The words clamoured disingenuously in the wind, lashing Chadaev with cruel and happy laughter. With equal force he lashed his horse and the sledge runners hissed more dejectedly in the beaten ruts.

All his life, to the envy of the world, luck had followed him, a reward for his insatiable hands. The year before being called up, he had married

the jolly Katerinka, and even in his ancient creaking house Katerinka's
noisy youth didn't fade. In the spring the windows filled with the ceaseless
whistling of starlings. Equipped with all that was necessary to cope with
life, the only thing Chadaev lacked was the gift of laughter. But even that
nasty short-change from fate turned out to his advantage: people were
afraid of him. The war spared his big body, red-haired, like a pine-tree at
sunset. He came home whole, without a wound. Then troubles, niggling
like mice, beset him. For a year he struggled with them, going crazy in the
fight, but they came in new waves to gnaw at his famous well-being. On
the days of respite he examined himself bitterly, failing to find the reasons
for his plight. Only now, as he headed for a final reckoning with fate, he
recollected one of his war adventures . . . and, although all sin is shameful
to a man if covered with a soldier's greatcoat, this particular memory
burned, bore a hole in Chadaev's being and refused to be erased.

At the time when the war was suspended and revolutionary freedom
raged, his infamous regiment had languished for half a year under the
southern sun. There Chadaev had got involved with a Moldavian woman,
a peasant like himself. She was as comforting as his own Katerinka, had
the same name, and she also pined for her husband, held somewhere
as a prisoner of war. She was attracted by Chadaev's restless northern
strength. He spent days and nights in her house under the acacias, ate
her chickens, drank her wine, held forth to his friends on the secret
charms of his Moldavian mistress. What was to him a passing fancy,
was her Moldavian love. He left her without regret, while the woman's
tears obscured from her the fact that, taking to the north her short-lived
happiness, he also took her sewing machine, which had caught his eye
in the hour of love. He could remember the seventeen rainy days he
had spent in a railway carriage in a typhoid haze, tightly clasping the
loot between his knees. It became more dear to him than bread and
life because he was taking it to his northern Katerinka, whom he had
placed in the centre of his imaginary happiness. But when one evening,
just as the cows were coming home, he climbed his porch in a hungry
sweat, swaying under the cherished burden, Katerinka had begun to cry.
Freezing, Chadaev stared at the crying woman with bleary eyes.

His illness and recovery revealed to him strange treasures which had
been outside his ant-like existence. He looked around him with almost a
seer's eyes, paying a tribute of non-peasant admiration to a flying insect
and a growing tree. But the peasant overcame the man in him. He spent
the winter doggedly mending his depleted holding, clearing the garden
and putting up so many starling houses it was as if he was trying to entice
happiness itself within his mouldy walls. But the starlings didn't stay, the

apples were eaten by worms and Katerinka's cheerfulness melted with the snow. Then, in confusion, he awaited children, but although dreamy people are fertile, there were none. Katerinka struggled like a wren against a bath-house window, went to visit the neighbours more often, looked older than her mother.

Then one time she had returned from haymaking radiant and young-looking. She had been quiet and spent the evening staring out of the window. At night, when everything belonging to Chadaev, the cattle and the chattels, was asleep, Katerinka laughed in her sleep. Climbing down from the stove where he slept, Chadaev watched her morosely, spread in her sleep and lit by the stealthy moon. However hard he peered into that tiny chink in Katerinka's secret, he saw nothing that night.

The rain stopped in the morning, sunny days followed and the lost smile returned to the house. When left alone with her thoughts Katerinka sang the maidens' songs of old and, although she didn't have the voice to sing them to the end, her husband felt an uncertain joy at her transformation. Once again prosperity visited the creaky house and the birds sang as if they were paid.

Chadaev drowsed like a mountain lulled to sleep by a breeze. Only his wife's last letter, an unexpected splash of someone else's happiness, disturbed his ponderous slumber. Dropping his business in the provincial capital, where he had come to petition for a cancellation of his arrears of food deliveries, he returned home as if to an inevitable grave.

His prediction had been true—even the dogs had gone to a dogs' wedding and nobody met the master. Tying his horse to the fence Chadaev stared intently at the vacant holes of the windows blinded by the sunset. An icicle under the eaves shed monotonous drops. Chadaev lashed at it crazily with his whip and waited some more, but his wife wasn't there. A boy sailing paper boats in a puddle shouted to him through the fence that Katerinka had gone to Serega in the new settlement. Chadaev started and looked around him: a neighbour's horse was scratching against a tree and calling for her foal; two women by the well openly watched his confusion. Just as he was, in a muddied coat and with the whip in his hand, Chadaev went to the new settlement. Once again his hands were outstretched, as if thirsting for an evil deed.

As he crossed the church hollow he kept wondering what qualities Serega had that had seduced Katerinka. He was a good-for-nothing dreamer who imagined a reform of the peasant economy with golden apples growing in a communal garden. In punishment for his aberration he had been demoted to a regional executive committee. He lived with his widowed brother, and copper Soviet wires hung on poles around their house. On winter evenings young people came to the house where they watched in reverential trance as Serega twiddled knobs on a home-made box and listened to unimaginable things happening in the world . . .

As he came nearer Chadaev smirked and threw sidelong glances at the ginger fire of sunset doused by the evening shadows. Women stood by the porch. They parted with a show of hostility. Chadaev's glazed eyes were more threatening than the whip squeezed in his mitten. Nobody dared follow him into the smoky darkness of the entrance.

First only purple circles swayed before Chadaev's eyes, but his heart sensed Katerinka's criminal presence. The silence seemed to tell him that something was wrong and, in suspicion, he shifted from one foot to another, hesitating to enter the stranger's home. His intuition proved right: early that morning Serega had been hit by a falling tree and now he was dying on a bench in the centre of the cottage. His yellow face, raised on a pillow, glowed ghostlike as if reflecting the large wax candle. He lay without movement, but fussy little currents ran through his body and his lips were open in a greedy bitter smile. To ease his suffering they had put the radio earphone to his ear, the only living thing in the twilight of the cottage. Chadaev saw his wife. Kneeling over her lover, Katerinka looked piteously at his face, her lips imitating every moment of his, as if she could hear everything at which he was smiling for the last time. This weird tryst had lasted since morning and even Chadaev didn't have the nerve to interrupt it. He coughed and Katerinka looked up. When she saw the whip in her husband's hand a severe shadow ran across her tear-stained face. Charged with the heat of Chadaev's hand, the whip moved and twitched, and it cost him some effort to suppress its vicious fervour. His eyes cast down, Chadaev approached his rival.

'No more running after girls, Serega . . . eh?' he asked sadly, offering forgiveness which the other man no longer needed. Serega stirred, his unsteady bruised hand pulling up the coat covering his mauled legs. 'Are you cold? You'll be cold while you're alive, then you'll get warm once you're dead,' Chadaev added earnestly and, marvelling at the force that restrained him, helped Serega to pull up the coat.

'Don't you scare him with death, he's worse alive than dead,' Katerinka said sharply, and the new cold blowing from her face made Chadaev shut his mouth. Then she clung fearlessly and piteously to her lost lover as if she were alone with him.

Serega seemed to be asleep. The earphone fell away from his cheek. Chadaev picked it up stealthily and pressed it to his ear. Empty space hummed hollowly in it and, by straining his whole being, he made out a distant murmur of trumpets coming in deep long sighs. The music was distant and mysterious, as if heard through a hundred closed doors, but it revealed Katerinka's secret much more clearly than that wild night. In superstitious fear he withdrew his hand, looking wildly around him. Nobody was watching him . . . and again, red in the face and sweating, he listened to Serega's scary and bewitching world. The music changed—an inhuman voice, insinuating and enticing, tempted Chadaev with the children fate had never given him despite all his prayers, with the horses he never had despite his passion for them, with everything that was dear to a human being on this earth. Shaking his head, scared by the magic promise of happiness, he ran out of the cottage, bumping into the woman doctor, brought by Serega's brother, on the porch.

Late at night the women brought Katerinka home and left her by the porch. From his stove Chadaev watched as, standing still for a while with her hands spread in misery, she collapsed on the bench. Black with love and humiliation, he sat down next to her. Transfixed with fear and expectation of pain, Katerinka looked at her husband's face disfigured by passion. Hardly daring to breathe, he leaned over and put his hands on her shoulders.

'My poor little bitch,' he whispered, suffering from the lack of other, more appropriate words.

She moved slowly away but, when the ginger wires of her husband's beard touched her temple, she jumped aside and screamed as if burnt. Taken aback by her scream, Chadaev stamped confusedly in the middle of the room, the flame of another wasted forgiveness billowing acrid smoke inside him. Then he walked unsteadily to his stove. Unlit for two days, it was cold and its cóldness filled his sleep with abrupt and weird visions. Among other things, terrible as an execution, he dreamed of the Moldavian woman. She stretched her hands to him with a pleading and wounding sound.

At daybreak sleet was falling outside the window. Katerinka was not in the house. Chadaev sat on the bench listening to something sighing in the cellar. He went out into the garden but the garden was even more unwelcoming and he returned to the house. Then Chairman Sorokin came with a warrant for a requisition of his arrears.

Chadaev had never had much time for this small man, who was like a polecat in his craftiness. He was always in a hurry, panting. He lived in constant annoyance, as if doing a vexing chore. Placing the warrant on the table before Chadaev, he told him to sign it.

'I can read print,' Chadaev said. 'But I can't write.'

'Just put a cross here testifying that you have read the warrant,' Sorokin said hoarsely. 'Tomorrow we'll distrain upon your holding.'

Their eyes met and they both turned away as if catching each other out telling lies.

'I'm in trouble, Sorokin,' Chadaev confessed, looking at the ridiculous wax seal on the skirt of the chairman's coat, which he had presumably obtained in a requisition. 'Serega's got into my bed.'

'What's the big deal?' Sorokin replied coldly, refusing Chadaev so much as the tiniest insincerity to relieve the distressing conjugal triviality.

'Katerinka's my wife, you know. For eleven years I carried her right here!' Chadaev cried, pointing to his neck for some reason. His beard fluttered like a bush on fire.

'What's the big deal?' Sorokin said with even more indifference, smoothing out the corners of the warrant.

'I loved her . . .' Chadaev said through his teeth, still trying to find a way to the official's heart.

Sorokin rose.

'What's your problem then? You're lucky. Serega died this morning. Now your Katerinka's all yours,' he said with a bored and angry face, and turned away, his fingers drumming on the window sill.

Chadaev sat bending low over the warrant and the paper stirred slightly in his breath. His first reaction to the news about Serega was joy, but then he thought of what was to follow, especially Katerinka's misery, and his enmity and jealousy of the two of them abated. The warrant swelled in his distracted imagination, reared up, fell on him, suffocated him. Obeying a strange impulse, Chadaev crumpled the paper into a ball, put it in his mouth and began to chew the nauseating thing before the eyes of the flabbergasted chairman. Then, staring vacantly at Sorokin, he swallowed it.

'You'll answer for this,' Sorokin said in confusion. He took a long time buttoning his coat and putting on his hat, as if giving the culprit a chance to repent.

'You're a smart one . . . but you've met your match,' Chadaev cried after him.

Chadaev found his bag and prepared for a journey. He broke a saucer and, although there was no hurry, didn't pick up the pieces. He went out. There was nothing left to keep him in that grave of disappointed expectations. The sun broke through the clouds but he was warm without it, with the rage he carried in his breast. He stopped at the gate and whistled to the dogs sitting by the well. They wagged their tails, danced on the spot in their canine confusion and stayed where they were. He called them by their names, patting his knee, but one of them turned its back to him while the other pretended to be examining a beetle. Chadaev left for ever.

First he went to his widowed sister in a nearby district and asked to stay, even as a farmhand. His sister, redheaded like all the Chadaevs and crazy with poverty, scolded him and gave him cabbage soup and a place on the sleeping bench next to her brood of emaciated children. There he spent his first homeless month, ploughing the earth and thanking his peasant God for ridding him of many unnecessary cares. But one day they caught up with him with a court summons and he had to disappear from his sister's in an unknown direction.

He could still move around freely, so he went to Porosyatnikovo for the haymaking. Conscientious in his new job, he did his best to justify his meagre keep. But soon the district secretary appeared in the meadow with a warrant for Chadaev's arrest. It was a busy time and they couldn't spare a man to accompany the criminal. Therefore a five year old girl, Aksyusha, was entrusted with escorting the villain the five miles to his just punishment. Chadaev laughed for the first time in his life, took the girl by the hand and set off.

They left when the dew was still on the ground. By midday the curly clouds in the zenith swelled, the stormy blue thundered and everything that grew froze in inexpressible melancholy. Chadaev and Aksyusha just managed to hide under a fir tree as the rain fell hissing on the parched fields. The girl was scared of the thunder storm. Shivering, she pressed against the tree and clutched Chadaev's hand. Sheltering Aksyusha from the fine spray, Chadaev began to tell her the stories his mother had told him in order to cheer up his own bleak childhood.

The stories were full of devils, stupid hairy troublemakers, one-eyed seers and, among other naive and obsolete ghosts, Ilya himself, the one who held thunder bolts in his hand like falcons. Chadaev had never spoken to anybody like that. The meaning of his story coincided with the fiery and thundery speech of the storm. Aksyusha listened to his wild fairy tale more attentively than to the frightening dialogue of the clouds.

Then the sun swept over the fields like a wide green wing, touching Aksyusha's bare feet. The rain stopped. The drops hanging on the branches and in the air sparkled. Near their feet in the grass a grasshopper chirped without fear of being squashed. Far away under the rainbow the dark insatiable belly still rumbled.

'You're making it all up,' the girl said with a sly look as, remembering the grown-ups' joking orders, she pulled Chadaev on. The rest of the way to the town Chadaev didn't exchange a single word with his incorruptible escort, as if the recent danger of the thunderstorm hadn't brought them close.

Chadaev escaped from the district prison next morning. In a week he found a job as a forester.

The land to the south was treeless, and so every tree in Chadaev's reserve had a thief after it. The thieves were vicious in their struggle for their thieving rights. Chadaev's predecessor had had a stake driven through his sleeves. Then he had been set free to measure the forest with the stake. The forest was coniferous and unclean; its was rumoured that its stones sang in the autumn and its firs walked from place to place. If there was no forester in it. Chadaev was the man for the job. His very existence, senseless as it was, scared off the thieves. The thieves would have remained without work and their children without food if, one evening, as Chadaev sat barefoot by a ditch watching tadpoles dance in the red water, the bushes had not parted to reveal a policeman in full uniform with another warrant for Chadaev's arrest. Chadaev laughed and went into his lodge to put his shoes on. When the policeman, having waited for a long time, followed him inside, the lodge was empty except for a little owl whom Chadaev had picked up out of pity the day before. The owl sat on the table winking at the official, who reeled from the insult. Chadaev had vanished in the darkness of the forest.

Chadaev spent his first vagrant night on a pile of logs in a timberyard. The night was fragrant. He was woken up by a beetle who had crawled into his roomy nose. Birds dashed about in the air and a red-headed woodpecker, tired of hammering at a tree, watched the intruder pensively. Chadaev remembered the events of the previous day and laughed at the people who persisted in recording his crimes. Now, on top of his arrears and the eating of the warrant, there could be added failure to appear in court, evasion of justice and escape from prison. It was clear that he had estranged himself from the world for ever. Thus a tramp was born.

He didn't get attached to anything but existed in a state of constant motion. While he moved on, the world kept his record. It was not he himself which interested the world, but his crimes. Sometimes, bored with his idle solitude, he did odd jobs—a shepherd in the summer, a postman in the winter, a rafter in the spring. I met him one autumn by the river where I came looking for a herb I had heard of as a child. First I heard a strange plopping sound. Climbing down the bank I saw Chadaev engaged in what looked like sorcery. Lying on a raft and holding a log in one hand and a funny looking wooden scoop in the other, he patted the water with the log. After half an hour, when our mutual sniffing was over and he was assured that I didn't intend to administer justice to him, he explained to me laughingly how he caught sheat-fish. In calm weather his plopping could be heard from far away and the sheat-fish, curious to know what made the noise, came near and, as a punishment for its curiosity, ended up in a soup.

We sat by the fire. On the high river bank covered by bird cherry and aspen wood, the orange remains of the summer smouldered wistfully. My eyes smarted from the smoke but for some reason I kept throwing branches in the fire. Chadaev didn't mention his Moldavian woman but I had a feeling that he was thinking of her constantly and that one day he would humbly enter her courtyard where her husband would be smoking ham. He would stand there for a while, attracting the husband's keen attention, then go away forever. However, Chadaev didn't confirm my fantasy.

'Another year and I'll turn into a proper devil. And what does a devil care!' the tramp said, and I imagined that he was a devil already, an animated horned prejudice. 'What does a devil care, I say! You can walk straight through him and he'll just laugh.'

The fish soup was ready but there was only one spoon. I left without finding my herb. The day was darkening, the trees became flat, the road lilac, the fields moist. I kept expecting to meet a horseman who would gallop past me brandishing a warrant for Chadaev's arrest, with orders to sew him into a sack and bring him to the district capital for interrogation. At that moment I almost believed a peasant legend about a bear who came out of the forest, bowed to the village near which he had spent his life, and vanished into the woods never to be seen again.

1928

Daniil Kharms
(1905–1942)

Kharms' real name was Yuvachev. His father, an intellectual and a revolutionary under the Tsars, wrote stories of fantasy; the son took after the father. Kharms was a notorious Leningrad eccentric in the 1920s, and in 1928 he became a member of the OBERIU group. His eccentric behaviour and absurdist writings did not go unnoticed and Kharms, together with his friend the poet Vvedensky, was arrested and executed. Apart from a few stories for children, Kharms' writings have never been legally published in Russia.

The following were written between 1930 and 1936.

The Trunk

A man with a thin neck climbed into a trunk, closed the lid behind him and began to suffocate.

'There,' the man with a thin neck said as he suffocated. 'I am suffocating in the trunk because I have a thin neck. The lid of the trunk is closed and doesn't let the air through to me. I'll suffocate but I'll never open the lid of the trunk. Gradually I'll die. I'll witness the struggle between life and death. The battle will be unnatural, with even odds, because in natural conditions the winner is death, while life, doomed to die, struggles with the enemy in vain, clinging to futile hope up to the last moment. In the struggle which will take place now, life will know by what means it can win; it will have to force my hand to open the lid of the trunk. We'll see who comes out on top! The only problem is that the moth-balls smell so terrible. If life wins I'll keep my clothes in tobacco instead. Here it comes, I can't breathe any more. I am dying, that's clear. I can't be saved. And there's no exalted thoughts in my head. I'm suffocating!

'Oh! What's this? Something happened just now, but I can't understand what it was. I saw something or heard something . . .

'Oh! Again something happened. My God! I can't breathe. I seem to be dying . . .

'What's this now? Why am I singing? My neck hurts . . . But where is the trunk? Why am I seeing everything that is in my room? I seem to be lying on the floor! But where is the trunk?'

The man with a thin neck got up and looked around him. The trunk was not to be seen. The things he had taken out of the trunk lay on the chairs and on the bed, but the trunk was not there.

The man with a thin neck said 'Life must have beaten death in a way unknown to me.'

The Dream

Kalugin fell asleep and had a dream in which he sat in the bushes and a policeman walked past the bushes.

Kalugin woke up, scratched his mouth and fell asleep again, and again he had a dream in which he walked past the bushes and in the bushes sat a policeman, hiding.

Kalugin woke up, put a newspaper under his head, in order not to wet the pillow with his dribble, and fell asleep again, and again he had a dream in which he sat in the bushes and a policeman walked past the bushes.

Kalugin woke up, changed the newspaper, lay down and fell asleep again. He fell asleep and again he had a dream in which he walked past the bushes and in the bushes sat a policeman.

Then Kalugin woke up and decided not to sleep any more, but he fell asleep at once and had a dream in which he sat behind the policeman and the bushes walked past.

Kalugin screamed and tossed in his bed, but he couldn't wake up any more.

Kalugin slept four days running and when he woke up on the fifth day he was so thin that he had to tie his boots to his legs with a string so they wouldn't fall off.

At the baker's where Kalugin always bought wheat bread, they didn't recognise him and slipped him rye bread instead.

The Sanitary Committee, making their rounds of the flats and seeing Kalugin, found him insanitary and useless, and they ordered the house committee to throw him out with the rubbish.

They folded Kalugin in two and threw him out like rubbish.

Anecdotes from the Life of Pushkin

1.

Pushkin was a poet and he was always writing something. Once Zhukovsky found him writing and exclaimed loudly, 'Don't tell me you're a scribbler!'

From that moment Pushkin took a great liking to Zhukovsky and began to call him in a friendly manner simply Zhukov.

2.

As is well known Pushkin could never grow a beard. This made Pushkin suffer greatly and he always envied Zakharyin whose beard, on the contrary, grew quite decently. 'With him it grows and with me it doesn't,' Pushkin often used to say, pointing his fingernails at Zakharyin. And he was always right.

3.

Once Petrushevsky broke his watch and sent for Pushkin. Pushkin came, examined Petrushevsky's watch and put it back on the chair. 'What do you say, brother Pushkin?' Petrushevsky asked. 'The machine has stopped,' Pushkin said.

4.

When Pushkin broke both his legs he took to moving on wheels. His friends liked to tease Pushkin and to grab him by the wheels. Pushkin got mad and wrote vituperative poems about his friends. These poems he called 'epigrams'.

5.

Pushkin spent the summer of 1829 in the country. He would get up early in the morning, drink a jugful of fresh milk and run to the river for a dip.

After taking a dip in the river Pushkin lay down on the grass and slept until lunch. After lunch Pushkin slept in a hammock. When he met the stinking peasants, Pushkin nodded to them and squeezed his nose with his fingers. And the stinking peasants bowed obsequiously and said, 'That's alright.'

6.

Pushkin was fond of throwing stones. Whenever he saw stones, he would start throwing them. Sometimes he got so excited that he would stand there, his face all red, waving his arms, throwing stones. It was simply terrible!

7.

Pushkin had four sons and they were all imbeciles. One of them couldn't even sit on his chair and kept falling off it all the time. Pushkin himself sat on his chair quite badly. It got really hysterical sometimes: they would sit around the table—at one end Pushkin would keep falling off his chair, at the other his son. Holy terror!

What they sell in the Shops these days

Koratygin came to see Tikakaev and didn't find him at home. At that moment Tikakaev was in the shop, buying sugar, meat and cucumbers.

Koratygin stood for a while in front of Tikakaev's door and was just about to write him a note when he saw Tikakaev coming up the street carrying in his hands an oil-cloth shopping bag.

Koratygin saw Tikakaev and shouted to him, 'I've been waiting for you a whole hour!'

'That's not true,' Tikakaev said. 'I've only been out of the house twenty minutes.'

'Well, I don't know about that,' Koratygin said. 'What I do know is that I've been here for a whole hour.'

'Don't lie,' Tikakaev said. 'Shame on you for lying.'

'My dear sir!' Koratygin said. 'Will you please watch your language.'

'I consider . . .' Tikakaev began but was interrupted by Koratygin;

'If you consider . . .' he said, but here Tikakaev interrupted Koratygin and said, 'You're a fine one yourself!'

These words made Koratygin so mad that he pressed one of his nostrils with his finger and blew out of the other at Tikakaev.

Then Tikakaev pulled a large cucumber out of his shopping bag and hit Koratygin over the head with it.

Koratygin clutched his head with his hands, fell down and died. They certainly sell large cucumbers in the shops these days!

The Cashier

Masha found a mushroom, picked it and brought it to the market. In the market they hit Masha on the head and also promised to hit her across the legs. Masha got scared and ran away.

Masha ran to the co-op store and wanted to hide there behind the cash register. But the manager saw Masha and asked, 'What have you got in your hand?' Masha said, 'A mushroom.'

The manager said, 'Aren't you clever. Would you like a job?' And he put Masha to crank the cash register.

Masha cranked and cranked and suddenly dropped dead.

The police came, made a report and told the manager to pay a fine, 15 roubles. The manager said, 'What's this fine for?' The police said, 'For murder.' The manager got scared, quickly paid the fine and said, 'Just take away this dead cashier at once.'

But the shop-assistant from the fruit department said, 'No, it's not true. She's not the cashier. She just cranked the cash register. The cashier is sitting over there.' The police said, 'It's all the same to us. We've been told to take away the cashier and we'll take her away.'

The police began to approach the cashier. The cashier lay down behind the till and said, 'I'm not going.' The police said, 'Why aren't you going, you fool?' The cashier said, 'You'd bury me alive.' The police began to lift the cashier off the floor, but they couldn't because the cashier was a very large lady. 'Lift her by the legs,' said the assistant from the fruit department. 'No,' said the manager. 'This cashier serves as my wife. Therefore I request, don't expose her lower body.' The cashier said, 'Do you hear? Don't you dare expose my lower body.' The police took her under the arms and dragged her out of the shop.

The manager told the assistants to clean the shop and commence trade. 'But what are we going to do with the body?' the assistant from the fruit department said, pointing at Masha. 'Heavens above,' said the manager. 'We've got them mixed up. Indeed, what are we going to do with the body?'

'And who is going to sit at the till?' the assistant asked. The manager scratched his moustache and said, 'Ha-ha! It's not that easy to stump me. We'll put the body at the till. Maybe the public won't notice who's sitting there.'

They put the dead woman at the till with a cigarette between her teeth, so she'd look more alive, and put a mushroom in her hand for the sake of plausibility.

The dead woman sits at the till as if alive. Only her complexion is very green. And one of her eyes is open while the other is completely closed.

The Young Man Who Baffled the Watchman

'Well, I never!' the watchman said examining a fly. 'If you smear him with glue, it will probably be the end of him. Would you believe it? All it takes is a drop of ordinary glue.'

'Hey, you devil!' a young man in yellow gloves called to the watchman.

The watchman knew at once that the call was addressed to him, but he continued to examine the fly.

'It's you I am talking to!' the young man called again. 'Swine!'

The watchman squashed the fly with his finger and said, without turning his head towards the young man, 'What are you shouting for? I can hear well enough. There's no need to shout.'

The young man brushed off his trousers with his gloves and asked in a polite voice, 'Tell me, grandpa, which way do I go to heaven?'

The watchman looked at the young man, squinted one of his eyes, then the other, scratched his beard, looked at the young man again and said, 'Come on, don't loiter here, go away!'

'I am sorry,' the young man said. 'I have urgent business there. They've got a room ready for me.'

'Alright,' said the watchman. 'Show us your ticket.'

'I don't have a ticket. They said I didn't need a ticket to get in,' the young man said, looking the watchman in the eye.

'Well, I never!' the watchman said.

'Well?' the young man asked. 'Are you letting me in?'

'Alright then, alright,' the watchman said. 'You can go.'

'But where do I go? Which way?' the young man asked. 'I don't know the way.'

'Where do you want to go?' the watchman asked with a stern face.

The young man covered his mouth with his hand and said very quietly, 'To heaven.'

The watchman leaned forward, shifted his right foot for better balance, looked closely at the young man and asked sternly, 'What do you think you're doing? Playing the fool?'

The young man smiled, raised his hand in a yellow glove, waved it over his head and suddenly vanished.

The watchman sniffed the air. The air smelled of burnt feathers.

'Well, I never!' the watchman said, opened his coat, scratched his belly, spat on the place where the young man had stood and went slowly to his guardroom.

Joiner Kushakov

Once there lived a joiner. His name was Kushakov. Once he came out of his house and went to the shop to buy some glue.

It was thawing and the road was very slippery.

The joiner took a few steps, slipped, fell and bruised his forehead.

'Ho!' the joiner said, got up, went to the chemist's, bought a plaster and stuck it on his forehead.

But when he came out into the street and took a few steps he slipped again and hurt his nose.

'Ugh!' the joiner said, went to the chemist's, bought a plaster and stuck it on his nose.

Then he went out into the street again, slipped again, fell and bruised his cheek.

Again he had to go to the chemist's and stick a plaster on his cheek.

'I tell you what,' the chemist said to the joiner. 'You fall and hurt yourself so often that I suggest you buy a few plasters.'

'No,' the joiner said. 'I am not falling any more!'

But when he came out into the street he slipped again, fell and hurt his chin.

'Damn ice!' the joiner cried and ran back to the chemist's again.

'See what I mean?' the chemist said. 'You've fallen again.'

'No!' the joiner cried. 'I don't want to hear another word! Give me that plaster quick!'

The chemist gave him the plaster. The joiner stuck it on his chin and ran home.

But at home they didn't recognise him and didn't let him into the flat.

'I'm Kushakov the joiner!' the joiner cried.

'Tell us another!' they replied from the flat, bolting and chaining the door.